GOLDEN IDOLS

Book Three in the Angel Chronicles Series

ESTER LÓPEZ

Writing & Photographic Services LLC

For all the men and women who bravely put on the law enforcement uniforms to protect us from harm. And for Ben, who helped me with my research.

PRAYER OF PROTECTION

St. Michael, the Archangel, defend us in battle. Be our defense against the wickedness and snares of the devil. May God rebuke him, we humbly pray; and do you, Prince of the heavenly host, by the power of God, thrust into hell Satan and the other evil spirits who prowl about the world for the ruin of souls. Amen.

Most Sacred Heart of Jesus, have mercy on us (Three times)

THE ARMOR OF GOD

Ephesians 6:10-17

Finally, grow strong in the Lord with the strength of his power. Put God's armor on, so as to be able to resist the Devil's tactics. For it is not against human enemies that we have to struggle, but against the Sovereignties and the Powers who originate the darkness in this world, the Spiritual Army of evil in the heavens. That is why you must rely on God's Armor, or you will not have enough resources to hold your ground.

So stand your ground, with truth buckled around your waist, and integrity for a breastplate, wearing for shoes on your feet the eagerness to spread the gospel of peace, and always carrying the shield of faith so that you can use it to put out the burning arrows of the evil one, and then you must accept salvation from God to be your helmet, and receive the word of God from the Spirit to use as a sword.

"This one was different," Detective Elena Romero said. She pulled her binoculars out of the dusty white blinds and set them on the wooden desk facing the window.

"How so?" Detective Dave Tanner asked. He sat at the same desk, his feet propped on top. He leaned back in the sturdy wooden chair and balanced his weight on the two back legs. He cradled his third cup of coffee in hand.

"She was very specific about the time and place," she said, sipping her coffee. An opened box of Krispy Kreme donuts sat on the table between them in the dark room. She glanced at her watch with the light streaming through the blinds from the street lamp outside. 4:43 a.m. She moved the blinds apart with her fingers and glanced down at the jewelry store across the road. Something moved.

She slammed down her coffee cup and grabbed the binoculars.

Tanner jerked his feet off the table, spilling his coffee.

"Damn." He grabbed the radio.

"It's going down!" she said. She jerked the binoculars out of the blinds and set them on the desk.

"There are two of them, just like she said."

Tanner keyed the mic on the radio. "This is Unit 19, we have a robbery in progress and need a backup on the corner of S.W. 8th Street and 37th Ave." He slipped the radio into the holder on his belt, and checked his gun.

"You ready?" she asked. She checked her gun as well, then slipped it back into her hip holster. The bulkiness of her bulletproof vest under her t-shirt made it uncomfortable to wear a shoulder holster.

"Yeah, let's go!"

She bolted out the door of the small office and took the stairs two at a time. Her heart pounded. She could feel the adrenaline pump through her veins. Tanner was behind her.

Quietly, she slipped out the front door of the drugstore and used her '67, candy-apple red mustang parked out front for coverage. She pulled her Glock out of her holster and wrapped her free hand around her other hand for support. She brought the gun to rest on the side of the trunk. Tanner was beside her, peering through the car window to the store across the street.

"You take the first guy, I'll take the second," she said.

Seconds later, the two suspects emerged from the jewelry store.

"Freeze! Police!" she yelled. She stepped out from behind the car, her gun pointed at the chest of the second perp. The first perp dropped the duffle bag he held and ran down the street. Tanner was after him.

She moved toward the second perp. "Get your hands up where I can see them," she yelled.

He dropped his bag and raised his hands. "Don't shoot! Don't shoot!" he screamed.

"Don't give me a reason. Up against the wall," she said. She closed the distance between them.

He lowered his arms a little, trying to get a better look.

"If you want to keep that pretty face intact, get those arms up high," she yelled.

He hesitated. Big mistake. She stuck her gun at his temple and shoved him face first toward the wall. "Two things I hate most in this world are thieves and liars." She kicked his legs out to put him off balance. "I especially hate thieves who lie."

She slipped her weapon back into the holster and patted him down for weapons. She found something hard on his leg, near his boot.

"Oh, this is good," she said. She pulled a sheath knife out from his boot and tossed it away. "Hands behind your back."

He did as he was told and she had him cuffed when she heard a gunshot. *Oh God.* She took a second pair of cuffs and locked the perp to the street lamp nearby.

"Hey, this hurts," he said.

"Get used to it." She ran down the street to where Tanner had gone. *Please be okay. Please be okay.* She pulled her Glock out of the holster once more.

She was suddenly aware of the silence. *Where's our backup?* When she got to the corner, there was Tanner, on the ground. She felt for a pulse. He was alive. She found the radio.

"Officer down. I need a backup. Suspect is on the loose. This is Unit 19 at the corner of S.W. 8th Street and 37th Avenue."

"10-4."

Another gunshot went off near her head. She dropped the radio beside Tanner, and ran for cover. Her eyes adjusted to the darkness of the alley. She moved toward where she had seen the flash and something hit her in the face, hard. She fell to the ground. Her gun flew out of her hand.

Oh God. Not that. She felt around and thought she found her weapon, when it moved. *It was a man's foot.* She hung on as he dragged her across the pavement. The ambulance's red lights struck him from behind as he kicked free, but not before she noticed the left heel of his shoe was two inches higher than his right.

She was up and after him, but he was gone by the time she got to the end of the alley. She returned to where she had lost her Glock as the backup unit pulled up next to the ambulance. She borrowed a flashlight from one of the officers.

Her face throbbed and her lip felt swollen from where the perp had hit her. She found her weapon and checked the safety. She returned it to her holster.

"How's Tanner?" she asked the EMT.

"It doesn't look good." The two EMTs loaded Tanner onto a gurney and into the van. She needed to call his family. *God, please help Tanner. Let him be okay.*

After the ambulance left, she noticed all the blood on the ground. That didn't look good at all.

One of the officers escorted her back to the other perp.

"We found Tanner's gun. The perp must have taken it from him and shot him with it. You'll need that for evidence." He handed it to her in a baggy.

She stopped long enough to call Tanner's parents, but a heaviness in her heart nagged at her the whole time. *Why did it have to happen to Tanner? We got along great.* Her lip hurt and she could still taste the blood in her mouth.

Another backup unit pulled up next to the jewelry store where the second perp was detained.

"Detective Romero?" an officer from the second backup asked.

"Yes?"

"I've alerted the tech team. They're on the way."

She gave the officers a description of the suspect that got away and they took the other suspect into custody. Another unit stopped by and they continued to patrol the neighborhood, trying to locate the first suspect.

She returned to the drugstore across the street and retrieved her binoculars and the leftover donuts after cleaning up the mess from the coffee.

"Here you go," she said. She handed the donuts to the officers still helping on scene. Then she tossed the binoculars inside her car and locked up at the drugstore.

She continued to work with the tech team to collect the evidence. By the time they finished, it was sun up. Now her day was officially starting.

When she got to the office to write up her reports, the captain approached her desk.

"Can I see you for a moment?" he said.

"Yes, sir." She hoped Tanner was all right. She slipped her purse into her desk drawer and followed the captain into his office.

"I got word from the hospital that Tanner is in ICU. The bullet hit him above the vest."

"Oh no." *God help him. Tanner had to pull through.* She made the sign of the cross and said a quick prayer.

"What happened to you?" He pointed to her face.

"I think the perp hit me. It felt like a fist, anyway."

"Finish up your reports and take some time off."

"I'll be fine, sir. I'd rather finish this investigation. It'll help me keep my mind off…Tanner."

"I can't let you go out there alone, Romero. You need a partner."

The phone rang and the captain answered it. "Hello. What? Yes. Yes, that's fine. Send him in."

"Go finish your reports and get some ice on that lip. You look like a prize fighter," he said.

That bad? She'd have to visit the ladies room to check on her injuries.

As she headed out the door, she passed a tall, good-looking man she had never seen before. He wore a Stetson. The look on his face was one of surprise. The Miami-Dade Police Department was a big place.

He tipped his hat and nodded in passing. He wasn't in a uniform, but then again, neither was she. The man had on boots and reminded her of a cowboy. *A cowboy in Miami?*

She headed to the ladies room. *Oh my gosh!* No wonder the guy looked surprised. Her eye was so puffed up, it was almost closed. Her lip was swollen and split. She wet a paper towel and dabbed at her face. "Ouch!" *That was a dumb idea.* Well, she couldn't wear a bag over her face and she had work to do.

She headed back to her desk and worked on the reports until her eyes burned from the strain of being up so late. It was barely 9:00 a.m., but she had been awake since midnight for the stakeout, with only a four-hour nap before that.

She could never go back to graveyard. That was the worst shift, trying to stay awake and turn her whole life upside down.

After finishing the paperwork, she headed to the captain's office.

"Here are the reports, Captain." Now her jaw hurt when she talked. She handed the papers to him.

"I've got you a temporary partner," he said.

"Who?" No one else wanted to be her partner, that's how she ended up with Dave Tanner. He was new in the department and single.

"A new guy on loan from Broward County."

"What?"

He glanced at his watch. "He should be here any minute.

There was a knock at the door.

"Punctual. Come in," he called out.

And there again was the tall, handsome man she had seen earlier.

Oh boy.

He handed her a zip-locked bag with ice in it.

"What's this?" she asked.

"For your lip. Captain's orders."

"Romero, this is Pete Cummings, your new partner. Fill him in on the investigation.

The dispatcher came on the radio. "Captain, a robbery just went down at the Metro Museum and there aren't any investigators available."

The Captain shot a glance at the two of them.

"I'm already on overtime, Captain," she said.

"Take a comp day later this week. Get on that and report to me before you leave."

"I'm driving," she said, walking toward the door. She slipped her cross-body bag over her head.

"Says who?" Cummings asked.

"I outrank you and you're just a rookie."

He held the door for her. "I'm driving because you need to take care of that lip. You think people are going to feel safe around someone who can't defend themselves?"

She stopped in her tracks. *Who the hell does he think he is?* She turned to glare at him. "That was rude!"

"Have you even seen your face?"

"Yes, and there's nothing I can do about it. We have a job to do. You can either go with me or stay here. I don't care."

She continued to the parking lot. *Why did the captain give me an ass for a partner?*

"Whoever hit you had a strong right hook. You've got a black eye and a swollen lip. I'm driving while you apply the ice and hope the swelling goes down before someone else sees you."

This wasn't going to work. This guy was already on her 'do not like list' and she didn't even have a list.

She put on her sunglasses and held the ice to her lip.

"Ouch." The sunglasses and the ice both hurt. *What the hell?* She glanced down at her clothes. Her shirt was torn and pitted where the perp dragged her. At least her bulletproof vest protected her skin from abrasions.

"Let me grab a change of clothes from my car." She motioned to her car, which wasn't far. *Maybe I'll let him drive. This time.*

"We don't have time." He stopped in front of a giant pickup truck. The kind you need a ladder to get to the step.

Cummings opened the door for her. Maybe he was making up for being so rude.

"Thanks," she mumbled. Once inside, she reached up for the visor to check the mirror. She lifted the sunglasses and saw her left eye was now bloodshot and more swollen than before. Her lip was still puffy, with greenish purple bruising showing up on her tender jaw. She noticed dried blood on her face. She wet her fingers and wiped off the blood the best she could.

Cummings had climbed in when she shoved the visor out of the way.

"Thanks for the ice," she said. She held the bag against her mouth. It looked much worse than it felt. Maybe not. It felt pretty bad.

Cummings drove out of the parking lot.

"Do you even know where the museum is?" she asked.

"Yes."

The two drove in silence for a few minutes.

"So you live in Broward County?" she asked.

"You could say that."

Hmmm. *A man of few words.*

"How long have you been on the force?"

"Not long."

"So what did you do before this?" *I'll get him talking one way or another.*

"I trained warriors and guardians."

"What kind of warriors?"

He glanced at her. "People who go into battle, kind of warriors."

"That sounds intense. What made you choose the police force?"

"It's a temporary assignment."

"Oh, until you make full detective?"

"Something like that."

This guy was closed up tight. Tanner liked to talk. He could talk about anything. And he was nice. She wasn't sure about this guy at all.

She leaned back against the seat and kept the ice on her lip. She must have closed her eyes for a few minutes because when she opened them, they were at the museum.

Cummings got out first. Before she could get down off the step, he was there by the door and handed her his dress shirt.

"Put this on. It'll look better than that worn-out t-shirt you've got on."

"It wasn't worn out when I put it on yesterday." She handed him the bag of ice, then slipped on his shirt.

"A little big, don't you think?" She stood there with her arms out. Cummings handed her the bag of ice and started rolling up her sleeves.

"I could have done that, you know. I'm not helpless." She felt like a stuffed olive with her bullet-proof vest under her worn-out t-shirt, covered with a man's dress shirt.

Cummings looked good with his snug-fitting, white t-shirt, covering some hefty biceps, tucked into his jeans. He definitely looked like the cowboy type. She wondered what he looked like without a shirt.

"Are you sure you're from Broward County?"

"I'm not from around **here**," he said.

"You certainly don't look like it, that's for sure." She grabbed her pad and pen from her back pocket and headed inside. He stopped her.

"Just a minute." He lifted her chin with one hand and with the other, ran a finger over her swollen lip. She could almost feel the swelling go down. *Maybe I just imagined it?*

"What was that about?" she asked.

"You had something on your lip."

"Oh, thanks." *Probably the blood I missed.* The sensation from him touching her felt odd to say the least.

She noticed there were two police cruisers in the parking lot, with the entrance cordoned off. The tech team was there as well.

Just before they got inside, she grabbed his arm. "When you interview people, pay attention to what they say as well as what they don't say," she said.

"I think I know how to interview people," he said.

"I don't doubt that. We are investigating a robbery and we need more detailed information than you would normally take in a police report. Every detail matters," she said.

"Now wait a minute! I always take good notes." *Do you think I'm sloppy?* he thought.

"I didn't say you were sloppy," she said.

"What?"

She glanced up at him with a scowl on her face. "Let's go, then."

Cummings pulled the door open and let her enter first. Inside, there were groupings of paintings on all the walls, with display cases under each of the groupings. In the center of the room, there were four large display cases. The base of each was made of wood, the sides and top were of glass. Three of the four central cases were intact. She took notes of what she saw.

In the center of what used to be the fourth display case was a large tin pail. It was half full of soapy water. Broken glass and soapy water were splattered all over the floor. A rag mop lay on the floor near the case.

Inside the case, the pail rested on a black velvet cloth that covered the entire shelf. There were imprints in two places where objects had been.

She introduced him to the tech team. "What have you got, Keith?" she asked.

Keith stood up from his work on the floor. "It looks like we got some good prints."

"So what's missing?"

"Two rare Mayan artifacts were stolen. They were on loan from the Mexican government. They're worth millions!" he said, in a lowered voice.

She scribbled some notes in her pad. "Where's the owner of this place?"

"The manager is over there," Keith pointed.

"Why don't you go interview the guards, Cummings, and I'll interview the manager."

"Sure, whatever you say, Detective Romero."

This was going to be more difficult than training warriors or guardian angels. They never questioned his authority and always did what he commanded. He wasn't used to taking orders from anyone, except Raphael, of course. At least now he had something to do. But earlier she responded to some-

thing he thought. Did she hear his thoughts? Was that possible?

He walked toward the guards and introduced himself, while manifesting a pad and pen. He took statements from the guards, interviewing each of them separately. From a distance, he could see Romero, along with her Guardian Angel, Lia. He had trained her years ago. Romero seemed professional enough. It was good that he healed her face before they walked inside. He couldn't have her look like a victim of domestic violence while performing her job. However, his shirt looked a little comical on her, but it was better than her torn t-shirt.

He walked toward the two police officers and saw the manager hand Romero a brown envelope.

"These two gentlemen are eyewitnesses to the man they suspected of breaking into the case," he said to the officers.

"I need you to take them downtown and have them look over some mug shots. See if they can identify the suspect." He jotted down the officers' names and then spoke to the two guards again, letting them know what was about to happen.

He rejoined Romero while she spoke to a short, Hispanic woman with flaming red hair.

"I'm Lieutenant Elena Romero, with the robbery division." She flashed her badge. She glanced up at him and introduced him as well. "This is Detective Cummings, my...partner."

"I work over there, behind this building." Her accent was thick. "I open the blinds in my office, when a dark green car pull up outside the museum. Then I hear the alarm. A man run out of the museum from the back. He carry a small, red bag and get in the car and drive away."

"What did the man look like?" Romero asked.

"The driver, he have...eh, how you say? A mostacho?"

"A mustache?"

"Si."

"And the other man?" he asked.

"No mostacho. Dos hombres have dark hair."

"Are you sure?" Romero asked.

"Si."

"Did you see the color of their eyes?" Romero asked.

"I no see the eyes. Too far."

"What about the car? Did you see what kind of car it was?" Cummings asked.

"No. It was old and green, that's all."

He placed his hand on her shoulder. "Can you picture the car in your mind for me?" When she did, he saw it as well.

"Thank you."

Romero glanced up at him with a questioning look. He ignored it and made some notes.

Romero handed the woman her business card. "Call me if you think of anything else."

"Gracias."

Romero walked over to the tech team. "Did any of you see a green car around here?"

"What kind of green car?" Keith asked.

"A Ford Fairlane," he said.

"How do you know it was a Ford?" Romero asked.

"I just know," he said. *He couldn't explain that he saw what the woman pictured in her mind.*

Romero pulled out her cell phone and called the dispatcher. She gave a description of the vehicle and a vague description of the suspects for an All-Points Bulletin, or APB.

"Let's get back to the station," she said.

"Yes, Detective Romero," he said. He didn't like being bossed around.

She glanced up at him. "Since we're going to be working together, you can call me Romero or Elena, okay?"

"I don't have a problem with Detective." *But I do have a problem with your attitude.*

"My attitude?" She put her hands on her hips. "You are a temporary partner, buster. And if you don't like working with me, I can fix that." She headed for the door.

He raised his hat and scratched his head as Lia followed behind Romero. *'She's very intuitive,' Lia called out over her shoulder.*

Is that what it's called? And she heard his thoughts again. How was that even happening? He could hear Lia's thoughts because they were both spirit beings. He just happened to be in human form at the moment.

While Cummings drove back to the station, Elena pulled the visor down.

"I had the strangest feeling earlier," she began. She lifted her sunglasses and noticed her eye was back to normal. No swelling. And her lip was also back to normal. All the bruising was gone. Her eyes widened. "Oh my gosh! I'm healed!"

She turned toward him. "How did you do that?"

"Do what?" Cummings kept his eyes on the road.

All her thoughts came together. He healed her. He saw the vehicle the woman had seen. She heard his thoughts. He trained warriors and guardians.

"You're an angel?"

4

Cummings pulled into the parking lot of a Waffle House and turned toward her.

"How do you figure I'm an angel?" He half turned toward her with one hand on the steering wheel, the other on his hip. He tensed his jaw.

"You train guardians. The only guardians I've ever heard of were angels. Plus, you healed me. I know what I looked like before you touched me and this is healed." She pointed to her face. "Thank you, by the way. And besides that, I think I heard your voice in my head."

"I'm hungry. Let's go inside and talk." He turned away, reaching for the door handle.

She touched his shoulder and felt him flinch. "Are you going to admit it, then?"

"Admit what?" He stopped and put both hands on the wheel, staring straight ahead.

"That you're an angel. Why are you here?"

He closed his eyes and took a deep breath. "Yes. I'm an angel. I'm on a special assignment."

"Am I going to die?"

"Why do you think that?" He turned toward her.

"Because I've heard of people who saw angels and it was on their death bed. My abuela saw angels and my abuelo who had died years before…moments before she died." She choked on those words, the memories still fresh in her mind.

"Eventually, when you are much older. Like most people, you'll die of old age. I'm here to prevent that from happening now."

She touched her chest. "What do you know that I don't?"

"I only have information as it is needed, in your case. Let's go inside. Being in this form makes me hungry."

"Sure." She opened the door to climb out and there he was.

"Boy, you're fast." She stepped down from the truck and he locked it up. They headed inside.

She had a lot to process. And plenty of questions.

After placing their orders, he pulled out his pad and pen. Romero touched his hands to stop him. Each time she touched him, a little shock went through his body. Was that normal for humans?

"How long are you here for?" she asked. Her eyes pleaded for an answer.

Her hands were warm and the tiny sensations he felt were definitely new but pleasant. Being in human form this long was also new to him. He didn't realize all the sensations humans felt when touching another human. That could be why he was warned not to stay in this form for long. Animals were much easier.

"As long as it takes."

"As long as what takes?"

"I'm here to help you with this case."

"Which case? I have two ongoing cases now."

"You'll have to figure that out yourself, I can't interfere with free will."

"Are you here as my partner?"

"For now, yes."

"Then that means you will help me figure this out, right?"

He closed his eyes momentarily. She was much smarter than he anticipated.

"You got me, there."

"Good." She patted his hand.

Just then, the server brought them some coffee. She took her time pouring the coffee while staring at Cummings. Finally, she left.

"What have you got on the guards?" she asked.

He flipped open his pad and glanced at the notes. "They were making their rounds when they noticed the janitor was not the regular guy. The replacement was mopping the floor when they walked down the hall. When they got to the end of the hall, they heard glass breaking. The two of them ran back to the central cases, just after the alarm went off. He was gone by the time they got to the door. They didn't see how he got away."

"Follow up on the replacement janitor," she said.

He raised a brow. "Are you telling me what to do?"

"You are a rookie detective, are you not? Check the agency that the regular guy worked for and find out who his replacement was. Oh, and have the guards go downtown to look at mug shots."

"I've already taken care of the mug shots part."

"Very good." Romero sat back in her seat, her arms crossed.

The server brought their food and set it down. She looked

at Cummings. "I haven't seen you here before, cutie, what's your name?"

"The name's Pete." He took a sip of his coffee.

"I'll be right back," the server said.

"We'll be right here," Romero blurted out, sarcastically.

He spewed his coffee all over the table.

She was quick with the napkins, sopping up the mess.

He wiped his face and tried to hide a smile.

"A little jealous, are you?"

"Of what?" Her brows knitted.

"My mistake."

"First we eat, then we talk," she said.

"Fine." He was hungry and the smell of food didn't help the situation with his stomach.

Soon afterward, Romero opened her purse and pulled out a folded brown envelope and set it on the table.

"Here's what I have on the museum manager," she said. She pulled out her pad and flipped it open. "His name is Jay Kleinman. He had some photos of the artifacts that were stolen."

"Let's see them."

She pulled out two 5 x 7s from the envelope and handed them to him. He studied the images.

One was a small, skeleton-like face, with a smiling mouth, full of teeth and made of pure gold. The object wore an elaborate headdress, almost as wide as the large, collar-like shield of intricate designs. Around the neck there were three chains. The bottom chain had an amulet.

"It was a piece of Mayan jewelry, made of pure gold," she said.

"Which one?" He was confused about where she was going with this.

Romero moved into the seat beside him, putting her arm on the back of the booth, her body against his arm.

"This one," she pointed to the one he had been studying.

She was so close he could smell flowers in her hair. That same feeling came back, only stronger. Her hair had been pulled back into a ponytail earlier and now was slowly coming apart. Loose curls fell around her face. She glanced up and their gazes locked momentarily.

"Hey honey, I thought you were sitting over there." The server startled her.

"I changed my mind. Is that all right with you?"

He bit his lower lip to keep from smiling. The server filled his coffee and left hers untouched, then left.

"Well, we know who the teacher's pet is, don't we?" She glanced up at him.

He couldn't hold back and started laughing.

"It's good to know you have a sense of humor."

"Tell me about this photo," he said. He tried to refocus on the case.

"You can turn it upside down and either way, it looks like a face."

"It's ugly."

"This one is more valuable. It's the Mayan fire god and both pieces were on loan from the Mexican government."

"You know there is only one God," he said.

"Yes. I know, but because it's made of gold, it's more valuable. And the manager, this guy Kleinman, was sweating profusely this morning. Did you think it was hot in the museum?"

"No. It was actually chilly."

"That's what I thought. He was nervous about something."

"Wouldn't you be if you borrowed somebody's jewelry worth over a million dollars and it was stolen from you?"

"I would have had it insured." She rested her elbow on the table and tapped her chin with her fingers. "Something about him doesn't feel right. I think I'll call back and speak to the secretary. Maybe she knows something."

"Aren't we going to see the captain first?" he asked.

"Yes. And I have some work to finish up from my first case."

They headed for his truck. When they got to Romero's side, she took off his shirt and handed it to him.

"Thanks for helping me out this morning."

"No problem." He opened her door and headed for the driver's side. Once inside, she started with the questioning.

"Are you my guardian angel?"

"No, but I speak to her. She fills me in on things I need to know about you."

"So my angel is female?"

"Her name is Lia. She's been with you since you were born."

"Cool. So why isn't she helping me?"

"She helps you all the time. She says you actually listen to her most of the time."

"That's good, isn't it?"

"Yes. But God sent me to help you with this case."

"So I have help from two angels, then?"

"You could say that, yes."

"Will I get to see her?"

"Only if she wants you to."

"So, did God give you any special instructions concerning me?"

"Of course he did. He wouldn't have sent me if you didn't need my help."

"What did he say?"

"He gives me instructions as we go."

"Have you seen God?"

"Yes."

"Well, what does he look like?"

"He's a spirit being without form, but you can imagine him any way you want."

"Are you all shape-shifters?"

"Of course. We can take many forms."

He pulled into the parking lot of the station. Hopefully, she'd stop asking questions.

"How many times have you been human?"

"This is my first time."

5

"The captain is in a meeting," Cummings said, hanging up the phone. He sat at Tanner's desk, facing her.

She thought about Tanner and how he had tackled problems with her in the past. She said another prayer for his recovery.

"Well, I've got a prisoner to interrogate. You can come along with me or wait here," she said.

"I'm going with you."

The two of them sat across from the prisoner at a long table.

"Look, Henry was the only name he gave me," John Reese said.

"How long have you known Henry?" She asked.

"I just met him yesterday. He asked me if I wanted to make some easy money."

"So how much did you get out of it?" she asked.

"Nothing! I was supposed to meet up with him later this morning."

"What was your cut?" She scribbled some notes on her pad.

"I was supposed to get a $1,000 for helping him, but thanks to you, I got nothing." He slammed his fist on the table.

"Who was going to pay you?" Cummings asked.

She glanced at him. This was her investigation, wasn't it?

"Henry."

"What were you after?" she asked.

"He said I could have anything I wanted in the store. He was after some old necklace."

"How generous. Why did he want only a necklace?" she asked.

"I don't know and I didn't ask." He crossed his arms.

"Where were you supposed to meet Henry?" she asked.

"Some apartments in Little Havana. He was going to tell me where, but you spoiled everything."

"I'm so sorry about that Mr. Reese, but could you tell me what Henry looks like?"

"He's Hispanic, okay? Dark skin, brown eyes, mustache."

"Anything else?" Cummings asked.

She glanced at him again. *He's trying to steal my thunder.*

"Well, he's got acne real bad, you know, those scars people get from when they were teenagers?"

"About how old would you say Henry was?" she asked.

"Oh, somewhere in his twenties, I think."

"Mr. Reese, would you mind looking at some mug shots for me to see if you could identify Henry? I would appreciate it if you would," she asked sweetly.

"I guess."

She stood up and reached her hand out to Reese.

"Thank you, Mr. Reese. You have been so helpful, I will be sure and tell your lawyer how cooperative you've been. Thank you."

She went out the door and Cummings followed. She motioned to the officer they were done.

"Is it always that easy?" Cummings asked.

"No. He was very uncooperative earlier when I arrested him for armed robbery. He wanted to see his lawyer. Well, I spoke to his lawyer and found out this was his first offense, so I bargained with him. If he cooperated, I would lessen the charges."

"Maybe he will think twice the next time." Cummings said.

"I hope there won't **be** a next time!"

She saw Keith coming toward them in the hallway.

"Keith, what have you got for me on the jewelry store case?"

"Nothing. They must have been wearing gloves."

"What about the museum robbery?"

"We got positive ID on the museum suspect from the two guards. His fingerprints were on file and they matched the fingerprints we got from the scene. Come here and I'll show you."

She followed Keith to his office and Cummings followed her. Keith picked up some papers from his desk. "Here." He handed her the rap sheets.

Cummings looked over her shoulder. He stood so close she could feel his body heat. She realized how much taller he was when she felt him breathing onto her head. His nearness made her uncomfortable.

As she glanced over the papers, one had a photo of a Hispanic man in his twenties, clean shaven, smooth skin. His eyes were brown and his skin dark. The other page was a description. Ernesto Vasquez, 22-year-old Puerto Rican male. The rap sheet was long, but they were all petty thefts. Nothing big like the golden idols.

"Oh, here is his last known address." Keith pointed to it on the rap sheet.

She glanced at it. Greentree Apartments, Little Havana.

Cummings whispered in her ear. "Didn't Henry live in Little Havana, too?" The sound of his voice, coupled with his warm breath, sent shivers through her body. What was happening to her? She mentally shook off the strange feelings. "Yes, yes he did." She spoke in a whisper.

"Oh, I almost forgot," Keith said.

"What is it?" she asked.

"The owner of the jewelry store did say that something was missing."

"What was missing?" Cummings asked. His breath blew across her head.

There was that feeling again. Was it normal for an angel to give off this kind of vibe? Why was this happening to her?

"It was an old Mayan necklace."

❧ 6 ❧

After apprising the captain of the status of the museum case, she decided it was time to go home and get some sleep.

"I'm scheduled to work tomorrow at 8:00 a.m. I've been up since midnight, so I'm going home." She headed out the door of the Miami-Dade Police Department.

"Do you promise?" Cummings asked. He followed her out.

"Promise what?"

"To go home and go to sleep?"

"Of course." *Is he my Guardian Angel now?*

He held her gaze for a long time. "What? Don't you believe me?"

"From what Lia says, you don't know when to quit."

"Thanks, Lia," she muttered and rolled her eyes. *Of course, she was right.*

"I will follow you home to make sure." Cummings said.

Like I need a babysitter.

"I heard that."

Of course you did. "Wait. You heard my thoughts?"

"Yes. I can tune in when I want or need to. Apparently, you heard mine, earlier."

"Is that normal?"

"No. I don't know how you did that. But I can hear your thoughts if I so desire."

"How long have you been listening to my thoughts?" She shoved her hands on her hips.

"Just now, unless you want me to monitor all your thoughts?"

"No. I like my privacy. So stop doing that." She pointed a finger at him. She walked through the parking lot and got in her car. *What was he thinking, listening to my thoughts? Isn't that like eavesdropping?*

Once she was on the road, she realized the jewelry store was on her way home, sort of. She pulled over, along the curb. *I'll just run in and ask him about the missing necklace.*

She flashed her badge and asked to speak to the manager.

"That's me."

"What can you tell me about the missing piece of jewelry from this morning's robbery?"

"Actually, I have an extra photograph of it." He stepped into a back room and returned with a folder. "I photograph all my jewelry for insurance purposes." He handed her the black and white photo of the necklace.

"It was made of pure gold, which I thought was unusual for the Native jewelry I've seen," the manager said.

The necklace was a chain made up of segments. Each segment was intricately designed. One dangled from the center.

"In front of this center piece," the manager pointed at the photo, "there was a type of clasp. Something else must belong there."

"How did you come by this necklace?" she asked.

"It was brought in by an old man of Native decent. He needed money. I could see that it was valuable, so I gave him a good price for it."

"What insurance company do you work with?"

"Fidelity. As a matter of fact, Jay Kleinman, a friend of mine, recommended the company."

"Really?"

"Yes. Do you know him?"

"We met today. He had two Mayan artifacts stolen from the museum just after your break-in."

"The Golden Idols?"

"You've seen them?" she asked.

"Yes. He showed them to me the day he acquired them. He offered to buy my necklace."

"How much did he offer you?"

"Ten thousand dollars. I didn't take it, though, because I could see what he had was worth millions. That made mine more valuable."

"How so?" she asked.

"I think that one of those idols was part of this necklace."

"Thank you. You've been helpful. Here's my number in case you remember any other details." She handed him her card and left. *These two cases are getting more interesting by the moment and Jay Kleinman has some explaining to do.*

She jotted down the notes from their conversation and slipped her notebook back into her purse.

Little Havana was also on her way home. Sort of. It was a predominantly Hispanic neighborhood. Many of the old buildings were in need of paint. Some were painted in graffiti by local artists. There were store fronts as well as homes in the area with windows covered in wrought iron bars. It reminded her of a prison. In protecting their valuables from thieves, the owners locked themselves up in their own personal prisons. A lot of these places also had alarm systems and multiple locks.

On the street, children played with a ball. Cars were parked along one side. The ball bounced hard and hit one of the cars, releasing a piercing sound from the alarm system within the car. The children scattered, the ball forgotten for the moment.

Finally she found the Greentree Apartments. The tan paint on the building had peeled and cracked around the windows and trim. It was a two-story building with stairs at either end. A brown rail and walkway went across the front of the building from one stairway to the other. It reminded her of an old hotel.

The manager's door was brown, with 'Manager' written above it in black marker. She knocked. A gray-haired, middle-aged man opened the door.

"Yeah? What do you want?" he asked. He wore a dirty gray t-shirt stretched over a belly that looked ten months pregnant. His navy-blue pants came to five inches below the end of his shirt, exposing a hairy belly. He hadn't shaved in days.

"I'm Detective Elena Romero, with the City of Miami Police Department." She showed him her badge.

He looked her over, raising his eyebrows. She glanced down at what she wore and forgot she had on the torn t-shirt, dirty jeans, and who knows what her hair looked like?

"I'm looking for Ernesto Vazquez. Is he here?"

"No, he ain't here. I'm looking for him, too. He left two days ago and stiffed me for two months' rent."

"Do you know where he might be?"

"If I did, I'd have my money." He made a sucking noise at the side of his mouth.

"Can you let me into his apartment? I have reason to believe he was involved in a robbery this morning."

"Sure, but you ain't gonna find anything."

He unlocked Vazquez' apartment. The place was cleared out all right. No furniture, no clothes, nothing. She walked into the kitchen and snooped around, opening drawers and cabinets. Nothing but a few live cockroaches. She shuddered at the sight.

She opened the refrigerator. Nothing was in it, but something blue caught her eye under the corner of the door. She picked it up. It was a matchbook with Sweet Dreams Travel Agency printed in white on a royal-blue background. She opened the matchbook. Inside, under the phone number and written in ink was the name, Ramsey. She put it in her pocket.

"Thanks," she said to the manager and handed him her card. "If Vazquez shows up, call me."

She drove home, thinking about the suspects. What would they do with the idols? They couldn't fence them. Or could they? Right now, the idols were too hot to move. She would have to call some of her informants when she got home. She adjusted the mirror in her Mustang, then reached over and turned on the radio. The weather report was on.

"…a tropical depression in the Atlantic—" She switched the station to country music and thought about Pete Cummings. For an angel, he sure looked good. She had never thought about what angels looked like before. Why did he smell like leather? And why was she beginning to feel uncomfortable around him?

7

Cummings stopped by the Metro Museum. He knew Romero would be all right, even though she didn't go straight home. Lia kept him up to date. But it was imperative to get this information. The secretary was getting into her car when he approached. He remembered seeing her earlier.

"Hello. I'm Pete Cummings with the Miami-Dade Police Department." He manifested a badge and flashed it for her. "Is the manager still here?"

"Mr. Kleinman left early and didn't say where he was going or when he would be back. He told me to cancel all his appointments for the next few days."

"Do you mind if I take a look at his desk?"

"Well…" she hesitated. "I was just leaving."

"I promise I'll only be a couple of minutes."

She got out of her car and let him into the museum. There was a sign on the door that said 'Closed for a few days.'

"Everything has been so chaotic today, you understand."

"Yes, ma'am."

She showed him the manager's planner. Tomorrow's date

page was torn out from the book. There were some impressions left on the next page, however.

"Can I borrow a pencil?"

She rolled her eyes and found a pencil on her desk and brought it to him.

He ran the pencil over the impressions several times and came out with Kleinman's possible location. He tore it loose from the planner.

"Thank you!" He grabbed her shoulders and kissed her on the cheek.

"Well." She was pleasantly stunned.

"Oh, by the way, what insurance company do you use?"

"Fidelity. Do you want their number?"

"Yes, please. Oh and can you tell me who you hired to do your cleaning?"

The secretary brought two cards from her desk. One was for Fidelity, the other one was for Miami Janitorial Services.

"You've been a great help, thank you." He kissed her cheek again.

She touched her hair with her hand and smiled. "Any time I can help you, just let me know."

He smiled and left. When he climbed back into the truck, he realized he had no place to go, so he headed to Romero's home.

He mentally checked with Lia, and Romero was there, showering. She made two stops before heading home and ordered a pizza. When he got to her townhouse, he waited in the drive behind her Mustang. When the pizza delivery came, he stepped out and greeted him.

"Hello. Is that pizza for Romero?"

"Why yes. Are you Romero?"

He manifested some money to cover the pizza and a nice tip and handed it to him.

"Thanks man," the delivery guy said, then left.

Cummings walked up to the door with the pizza. He was hungry and Romero couldn't eat it all herself, anyway. He rang the bell.

When she opened the door, she wore shorts, a tank top, and her wet hair hung down past her shoulders. She held money in her hand.

"What are you doing here? Is that my pizza?"

"May I come in?"

She opened the door wider and stepped aside.

After she closed the door, he set the pizza on her coffee table.

"I see you didn't go straight home," he said.

"What?"

"I can communicate directly with Lia. You made two stops before coming home, didn't you?"

She glanced up to heaven. "Thanks, Lia. Yes, but they were sort of on the way home."

"Is this how you treated all your partners?"

"I shared my information with them. Before Tanner, I ended up doing most of the work myself. Tanner helped some. He just didn't like doing the reports."

He stepped closer to her, forcing her to look up into his eyes. "You need to share the load. You can't keep taking these cases on by yourself."

She closed her eyes momentarily. "You're right. I just want to be able to solve my cases. I give 100% but sometimes, my partners let me down."

"I'm your partner now. You can count on me. I need you to believe that."

"I want to believe that. But you're only temporary. What happens when you leave?"

"We will deal with that later. First we eat and then we talk," he said.

"Great idea. I have some drinks in the fridge, if you want one?"

"Sure."

She grabbed a couple soft drinks and opened them and brought out a couple plates and napkins.

"So, if you haven't been human before, is this your first pizza?" she asked.

"Mmm, yes!"

"And how's the drink?"

"Good."

Once they were finished eating, Romero cleaned up the mess and he got out his notes. She sat beside him on the sofa.

"I got a lead on the museum," he said.

"What's that?"

"Kleinman has left town."

"That's odd."

"That's what I thought."

"Well, I stopped by the jewelry store," she said. She stood up and went to her desk and picked up a photograph and the brown envelope and brought it to him.

He couldn't help notice her athletic build in her skimpy outfit. That's something he hadn't notice earlier with what she had on before.

He glanced at the image. "Is this the necklace that was stolen earlier?"

"Yes. I think our two cases may be related." She handed him the images of the golden idols.

"One of these idols could possibly be part of this neck-lace. We won't know that until we see the two idols."

"And what about your second stop?" he asked.

"I went to the Greentree Apartments." She handed him the matchbook.

"Sweet Dreams Travel Agency?" He flipped it open. Inside, 'Ramsey' was written in ink.

"I haven't had time to call them, but that may be their escape plan."

"Let me use your phone," he said.

She frowned.

"You do want me to help you, don't you?"

"Don't you have a phone?" she asked.

"No."

"You have a truck but not a phone?"

"Transportation is necessary, unless I teleport."

"You can do that? How awesome."

He held his hand out.

She handed him the phone and he placed the call.

"Yes, this is Detective Pete Cummings from the Miami-Dade Police Department. I'm calling to see if a man by the name of Ernesto Vazquez made a reservation recently. I believe he may be involved in a robbery. My badge number is 413. You can call the Miami-Dade Police Department to verify my ID." He hit the speaker so Romero could hear as well.

"Yes sir, he booked a reservation for a three-day cruise to Puerto Rico, but it wasn't for himself. He didn't have access to a computer, so he came in and paid with cash."

"Could you tell me who it was for?" he asked.

"It was for Juan Rodriguez, his uncle."

"Do you remember what Vazquez looked like?"

"He was Hispanic, tall, dark skin, brown eyes, a heavy smoker and he had a mustache."

"Thank you for your time. You've been helpful." He

handed the phone to Romero and noticed she was scribbling some notes.

"I also found out that the museum uses Fidelity insurance," he said.

She stopped writing. "Fidelity?" She glanced at him. "That's the same company that the jewelry store uses. In fact, Jay Kleinman suggested it to the manager."

"Interesting. I also got the name of the cleaning service. Did you want me to call them, too?"

"Sure, go ahead." She handed him the phone again.

While he dialed the number, she got up and left the room.

"This is Detective Pete Cummings from the Miami-Dade Police Department, badge number 413. I was calling to see who you sent to clean the Metro Museum yesterday? I'm investigating the robbery that took place there."

"Diego Gonzalez was supposed to go but he didn't show up for work and never called in."

"How long had he been working for you?"

"Several years. It was so unlike him."

"Can you tell me what he looked like?"

"He was Hispanic, middle-aged, about 5'7" and very friendly. He would talk to anyone."

"Thank you for your help."

Romero walked into the room, her brown hair dry and styled with a colorful scarf setting it off. *Very nice.*

"I was getting cold so I dried my hair. Find out anything?"

"The guy that was supposed to clean the museum didn't show for work."

"That doesn't help." She gestured for the phone. "I need to call the captain and let him know where we are in this investigation."

While she called, he hunted for a bathroom. Now that he

was in human form, he found some of these human necessities were bothersome. *How did humans deal with this all the time?* He thought about how much nicer Romero looked when she got cleaned up. It made him smile.

When he walked into the living room, she had just finished talking to the captain.

"I let him know about the travel agency. He's alerting the FBI to check all modes of transportation, plus we have that APB out for the car."

"So, what happens next?" he asked.

"We get some sleep, and tomorrow we tie up any loose ends. He's sending us on that cruise to see if we can apprehend this Ernesto Vazquez. The insurance company contacted the department about the robbery. They want this guy arrested. Maybe his uncle is the accomplice."

"A cruise?"

"Yes. You may want to pack some clothes. We'll be gone a few days."

"I, uh, don't have anything to pack."

"That's right. Where do you sleep at night?"

"Well, in spirit form, we don't sleep. But in human form, this body is getting tired."

"You never sleep?"

"In spirit form, no."

"Well, I've been awake since about midnight and I'm exhausted. You're welcome to use my sofa. I'd offer you the spare bedroom except there's no furniture in there."

"That's kind of you. I may take you up on it. As far as packing for a cruise, what will I need?"

"That's a good question. I've never been on one either. Maybe we can call them in the morning and ask. Where did you get those clothes?" She pointed to what he wore.

"I manifested them."

"What does that mean?"

"I thought them on."

"Wow, that must come in handy. Let me get you some sheets and a blanket. You can watch TV until you get tired but I'm beyond tired." She left the room and returned with an armload of things. He stood and watched her prepare the sheets on the sofa and then added the blanket and a couple pillows.

"I know you're way taller than me and this sofa may be short, but it's all I've got."

"I'll make it work. Thanks."

"I have an extra toothbrush you can have and some tooth-paste in the guest bathroom in there." She pointed to the room he found earlier.

He touched her shoulders and caught her gaze. "You've been very kind. I misjudged you earlier."

"That happens to me a lot, believe it or not. And it's not every day I get to entertain an angel." She winked. "Good night."

He sat down on the sofa and fiddled with the remote before figuring it out. He'd seen other humans watch these things, but he never had a need to in spirit form. He removed his boots and turned out the lights. After watching some random programs, he caught the weather.

"...tropical depression of the season. It's about 1,000 miles southeast of the Virgin Islands and moving fast." He turned off the TV and removed his jeans, then pulled the blanket over himself. This sofa wasn't bad. He drifted off to sleep, thinking about the woman in the next room and the approaching storm they would be heading into.

What exactly did you have planned for me, Lord?

8

Romero woke early and put on her dress pants and a nice blouse. Her usual for the office. She only wore the jeans for stakeouts, which weren't very often. While fixing her hair, she thought of Tanner. She had to call his family to see how they were doing and get the latest on his condition.

She headed to the kitchen for some coffee and breakfast. While pouring a cup of coffee, she heard a noise in the living room and spilled the hot liquid on her hand.

"Ouch!"

"You all right?" a male voice boomed through the room.

"Oh my gosh! I forgot you were here."

"Sorry to scare you." Cummings wore his jeans and t-shirt.

"Did you sleep in your clothes?"

"No, I just pulled on my pants when I heard you walking into the kitchen."

"Did you sleep well?" she asked. She reached into the freezer and grabbed an ice cube, rubbing it on her hand.

"Here, let me." Cummings approached her and took her

hand. He held it in one of his and placed the other on top. He closed his eyes.

She watched him and realized how handsome he was and how lucky she was to have an angel help her with this case. It must be important for God to send him to protect her.

He opened his eyes and she glanced at her hand.

"Wow, that feels better. Thank you."

He still held her hand. She glanced at her hand and he finally released it. His hand felt strong and warm.

"Would you like some coffee?"

"Sure. Thanks."

"If you want to shower and shave, I have everything you need in the guest bathroom, except clothes. Can you manifest something to wear?"

"Yes."

She handed him a mug of coffee. "Do you need cream or sugar?"

"I think I'll drink it black."

"Suit yourself. You don't know what you're missing."

"What do you have in yours?"

"I just use cream. Here, try a sip." She handed him her mug. He sipped it.

"You're right. I like it with cream."

"Here you go." She poured some cream in his coffee.

He drank it slowly. "Yes, this is so much better."

She reached out and rubbed his arm. "Go take a shower and I'll fix us something to eat."

He headed to the bathroom with his coffee. While he was gone, she prepared some eggs, bacon and toast. She felt a little excited, cooking for an angel. She realized her heart was beating a little harder. This was new for her but she liked how it made her feel.

By the time she had everything ready, he came back into

the room with dress pants and a dress shirt and tie. Her heart hitched.

"Wow. You clean up real good."

"Why, thank you. You do too." He smiled.

They sat together and ate breakfast.

"So, Lia tells me you rarely cook breakfast."

"Thanks, Lia," she said. "It's usually just me, so I don't cook much."

"This is good, Romero."

"Thank you, Cummings."

When they finished, she brushed her teeth and gathered her notepad and her cross-body bag to carry her stuff in.

"We'll have to take your truck or play musical cars," she said.

"Musical cars?"

"You can move your truck into the street so I can back out, and then park your truck in the driveway."

"Or we can take both vehicles," he said.

"Well, if we're going to be partners, we drive in one car."

"Good point. We take the truck."

She rolled her eyes. "This time."

She climbed up into his truck after he opened the door for her. *At least he has manners.*

They arrived at the station.

"Remember, we tie up loose ends and see if we can't get another lead," she said.

"I almost forgot." He turned toward her. "I got this lead yesterday from the secretary of the museum." He handed her the folded piece of paper.

She opened it. It read: C. Garza, Puerto Rico. Her eyes widened.

"What?"

"The night of the jewelry store robbery, we got an anonymous phone tip with the time and location." She pointed to the note. "It came from a woman in Puerto Rico."

"Let's see where this goes." He turned to get out of the truck. He still beat her to her side.

"Thank you. You're spoiling me," she said.

"How so?"

"I'm not used to men opening doors for me."

"Did you want me to stop?"

She touched his arm. "Don't you dare."

He smiled as they approached the station.

"Oh, I need to check on Tanner's family," she said, pulling out her phone.

"I'm going to grab some of that coffee."

"Get me some, too, please?"

Every time Romero touched his arm, he got that strange, pleasant feeling. It made him feel like touching her back. He thought better of it and kept his hands to himself.

He found the coffee station and poured two cups of coffee.

Another man approached, so he moved over to find the cream.

"You must be Cummings."

"Yes." He glanced at the man.

"John Douglass, Romero's first partner." He offered his hand so he shook it.

"What caused the breakup?" he asked while pouring the creamer.

"My wife, actually. After she met Romero, she made my life hell until I requested a change."

"What did Romero do, chew your wife out for something?" He took a sip of one of the coffees. *Romero's coffee was much better.*

"No, nothing like that. My wife was jealous."

"Jealous?" He remembered the scene from yesterday in the restaurant. She was good looking and the more he was around her, the more he noticed it.

Romero walked up to the coffee station. "I was wondering about that cup of coffee," she said.

"Here you go. Your coffee is much better," he said. He handed her the cup.

"You've had her coffee?" Douglass asked, his mouth hung open.

"Yes, I did."

She patted Douglass under the chin with the back of her fingers. "Close your mouth," she said. She and Cummings walked away.

"The captain wants to see both of us," she said. Together they went to his office.

"Come in, both of you, and have a seat." The Captain said. "Romero apprised me of your situation in your investigation."

Situation?

"I need you two to tie up loose ends. Romero will follow up with the agencies to see if our suspects have been spotted. I've notified the FBI. Cummings, you follow up on the museum janitor and the manager. You've got a couple hours to get this done, then go home and pack.

"Pack, sir?" he asked.

"Yes, didn't Romero tell you you're both going on this cruise, undercover, posing as husband and wife? Find the suspects, and keep an eye on them. The FBI will send someone there as well to apprehend them since it will be over international waters, but I want the department to get some credit for this arrest since you started the investigation." He glanced at his watch. "You better hurry. The ship leaves at 4 p.m."

Romero stood, so he stood and followed her out of the office.

"We need to talk," he whispered in her ear and pulled her arm. He escorted her to the elevator.

She gave him a scowl. "What's this about?"

"Something about this doesn't feel right." *Why was he feeling anxious? This wasn't normal for him. He could tackle anything. He'd faced evil spirits and won.*

"Like what? The actual cruise?"

"No, this husband and wife thing."

She laughed. "Is that what's upsetting you?"

"Yes. I don't know how to do that." He was used to training warriors. This was unfamiliar territory.

"Well, I've never been married but it can't be that hard. We just pretend that we like each other and hang out. Sort of like partners, only friendlier."

"Like partners?"

"Yes. You've got that part down, don't you?"

"Yes." He took a deep breath. "Okay." He had to calm down. Maybe it was as simple as being partners. "Okay."

"You actually looked worried." She touched both his arms and held them. "You can do this. We can both do this. We have to stop a criminal. That's the important thing. Let's get these calls made so we can pack. I'm a little excited. I've never been on a cruise before."

He nodded. "Okay." *Lord, why was he feeling this way? What was happening to him?*

9

He sat at his new desk, facing Romero. He called the Miami Janitorial Services once again to see if they had any news about their maintenance man. Nothing new there. Then he called the Metro Museum to speak to the secretary. The answering machine said they would be closed for several days. Nothing panned out.

Romero made her calls to each of the agencies, apprising them of the situation and the APB on the vehicle. It took a while. He waited for her to get off the phone.

"So what did you find out?" he asked.

"The descriptions of the two criminals are so similar, I thought maybe we were looking for one man with two accomplices."

"And we know who the accomplices are!" He stood up. "Let's have another talk with our friend, Reese."

Romero joined him as they walked down the hall.

"Did I tell you that Jay Kleinman wanted to buy the necklace that was stolen from the jeweler?" she said.

"Really? I found out that Fidelity is owned by someone named Carlos Garza," he said.

She stopped in her tracks. "Wasn't that the name on the manager's calendar?"

"Yes, it was."

Keith came down the hall and met them. "Hey, your friend Reese identified his accomplice."

"That's great news. Who is it?" she asked.

"Enrique Vazquez, brother to Ernesto." Keith said.

"That explains why their descriptions were similar," Cummings said.

"Well, his rap sheet was very different than his brother's. While Ernesto was into stealing, Enrique was into knives. He was recently released from prison for the rape and attempted murder of Carmela Garza. He cut her up pretty bad. If her husband hadn't found her when he did, she would have died." Keith handed her the rap sheet and the photo.

"Evil," Cummings whispered. She glanced at him, then touched his arm. *Is this the reason you are here?*

She heard another voice in her head say '*Yes.*' She glanced up at him. *Was that you, speaking to me?* He nodded.

Keith turned to leave. "Oh, they found the vehicle abandoned by the airport this morning. It was registered to Ernesto Vazquez."

"Great. Maybe they took a plane instead," she said.

"Do you think one of them left by cruise ship and the other by plane?" he asked.

"That doesn't make sense, does it? Maybe they abandoned the car to throw us off."

"It wouldn't hurt to make another call, would it?" he said.

"No. Let's do it." They headed back to the office.

After placing the call, she realized there were a lot of people with that name, but none by either Ernesto or Enrique bought tickets for today or this week. "Well, we're back to where we started. Let's go home and pack."

Cummings drove from the station back to Romero's townhouse. While they were driving, she got a call.

"Hello?"

"Romero? It's Keith. Just got word they found the janitor. He was in a dumpster, not far from the museum. In pieces. Be careful." She shuddered at the thought. She glanced at Cummings.

"What is it?"

"They found the janitor."

10

After manifesting enough clothes to fill a small suitcase, he and Romero drove to the Port of Miami.

"Oh, no." Romero said as they pulled up.

"What is it?"

"I just realized we didn't have time to change my passport. Mine is still under Romero."

"Is that important?"

"Yes. We'll have to board under our last names. You do have a passport, right?"

He glanced at her worried face.

"Can you manifest one?" She pulled hers out. "It looks like this, except it will have your image and your information on it."

He closed his eyes and one appeared in his hand. "Will this do?"

She took it from him and leafed through it, comparing it to hers. "I hope so. It looks just like mine except with your image."

"That's what you said, isn't it?"

"Yes, I did. Let's go."

~

By the time they got to the lines, Romero was fumbling with her purse and her camera bag.

"Let me take this," he said, grabbing the camera bag. "I'll wait for you at the end."

While he went through the line, he felt uneasy. He didn't like it one bit. The thought of Romero on the other side of this large room bothered him. He was supposed to be watching out for her. *'I have her back. She's in good hands.'* Lia's voice came into his head. Neither of them had weapons, although he didn't need one. But the Vazquez brothers could be here under disguise. Then it dawned on him: Rodriguez, Romero. He turned toward the R's. His heart pounded in his chest. This was new to him. He reached out mentally to Lia.

'He's here. Right behind Elena and very close. She feels it,' Lia said.

What do you need? How can I help you?

'Be still. I'll keep her safe.'

Now his stomach was in knots. How did humans deal with things like this? He wanted to be anywhere but here right now. He could pop out of this body, letting it fall limp to the floor, or he could teleport anywhere but here. At least they knew Rodriguez was here, but they didn't know if he was one of the Vazquez brothers or another accomplice. Somewhere on this ship was an FBI agent, so they must believe the brothers were here as well.

Finally, the line moved. They checked his camera bag and suitcase and sent him into another line.

~

Elena glanced around the warehouse-type building. It reminded her of the stock sales she went to with her abuelo, years ago. Instead of cattle, the place was full of people. Sweaty people, waving their little cardboard fans. *Yeah, like that would cool them off.*

The old man behind her was a little too close for comfort. He was taller and it felt as if he was breathing down her neck.

She turned toward him, gently pushing against his chest. "Do you mind?" He was bearded and gray and wore a hat and wire-rimmed glasses around brown eyes. His face didn't have the characteristic wrinkles of a man with gray hair, however. He smelled as if he had spilled an entire bottle of cheap men's cologne all over his clothes. He had a nice tan, though. Who didn't, living in south Florida?

They moved up in line. Her bags passed through the metal detector, but the old man was held up because he kept beeping. She noticed he had to take off his belt. She continued on in line, but a few minutes later, he had caught up with her.

When she handed the purser her ticket, the old man was beside her.

"Could you back off a little?" She stared him down. When he noticed the purser and another man glaring at him, he backed up a couple steps. "Thank you." She turned back toward the purser. He checked her name off the list.

"Your cabin is on the Twilight Deck, Ms. Romero. You can pick up your keys and a map on the Horizon Deck."

"Thank you." She noticed the other man was busy checking tickets as well, but a third man appeared to be looking over the passengers. Once inside, she headed for the purser's desk to pick up her keys. She didn't see Cummings anywhere. She turned to leave when she heard the purser say, "Juan Rodriguez?"

She glanced over her shoulder and realized the man who

had been behind her was Rodriguez, as the purser handed him his key.

Cummings approached the ramp and noticed a tall, Hispanic woman next to him. She wore a white wig, which made her brown skin look even darker. Along with that, she wore a pink dress and white heels. Her makeup was too heavy and she reeked of cigarettes.

When it was his turn, he set down his bags and took off his Stetson, pulling out his ticket from inside the band. He handed it to the purser. He noticed the Guardian Angels standing beside their charges. The one behind the third man spoke to him and said he was an FBI agent.

The woman next to him pushed ahead and shoved her ticket into the purser's hand.

"Yes, ma'am. You can pick up your cabin keys inside on the Horizon Deck."

She bent down to pick up her bags, bumping into Cummings with her hips. He noticed she had picked up Romero's camera bag. Before he could say anything, he noticed another camera bag just like it, next to his other bag.

That was close. He thought he would have to chase the woman down. He headed to the Horizon Deck after picking up his own bags. But Romero wasn't there. The purser said she had already picked up her key.

They were supposed to be partners. Why did she do that? He would have words with her.

When he arrived at the room, she was inside.

"Why didn't you wait for me?" He dropped his bags on the floor.

"I thought you might be here when I didn't see you."

"You've got to trust me. Rodriguez was behind you, wasn't he?"

Her eyes widened. "How did you know? Wait. Don't tell me. It was Lia?"

He nodded. "We've got you covered but you have to trust us."

She lowered her head. "This is hard for me. I'm so used to doing everything myself."

He moved to her and touched her shoulders and gazed into her eyes. "You have to use your faith and I know you have it."

"But you're only here temporarily. After you leave, I have to go on and I'll still have to do everything myself."

"What about Tanner?"

"Tanner is a good partner, but he doesn't pull his weight. I do most of the reports."

He let his hands run down her arms, holding her gaze. "You've got to trust me, Romero."

She closed her eyes momentarily. "I will try. Really."

He let his hands fall away from her arms. They were firm and muscular.

"I saw the FBI agent," he said.

"You did?" She moved to the bed and opened the suitcase. "What's his name?"

"His angel spoke to me. His name is Taggert."

Romero pulled clothes from her bag and put them into the drawers. Then she hung some of her clothes in the closet. "You might as well empty your bags since we'll be here a few days," she said.

He stood and watched what she did. He tried to repeat what she had done, but he had different items. "How do you know what goes where?"

She glanced up at him. "I'll help you. I keep forgetting

that all this is new to you." She showed him what items went into the closet and which ones belonged in the drawers.

"Promise me you won't go anywhere on this ship unless I am with you," he said when they finished.

"What?"

"Yes, you heard me. How do you expect to defend yourself against a man like Vazquez?" He approached her. "What if he came up behind you and grabbed you like this?" He turned her around so that her back was to his chest. His face was close to her hair. He wrapped his arms around her, grabbing her forearms as they were crossed in front of her. She smelled good. Her hair was soft. A warm sensation rushed through his whole body as he held her in his arms. She hesitated, then jerked her arms up hard and away and spun around, facing him.

"Very good." She impressed him, but broke the spell he was under.

"Normally, I would run away unless I had a weapon."

"What if he grabbed your arm like this?" He reached out and grabbed her forearm.

She jerked her arm down hard. "I would do this, and then run," she said, pulling away from him.

"What if he came up behind you and grabbed you like this?" He reached across her chest, grabbing her left upper arm. Romero jerked her left arm back hard, then reached up and grabbed his arm with both hands, twisting her body hard as she did, flipping him on his back on the floor.

He stared up at her, his mouth open. She could actually defend herself. "I'm impressed."

"Police training," she said, straightening her clothes.

He jumped up as if it didn't affect him.

"Had enough?" she asked.

He shook his head and backed her up against the wall.

"What if a guy like *me* came at you like this?" He took her hair in his right hand, gently pulling down on it so that her face was up toward his. He took his left hand and gently grabbed her right arm, pulling her toward him. Their lips were close. "What would you do?" He felt himself harden at their closeness. Something he hadn't expected. Then that feeling swept through him again and his heart pounded. *What was happening to him?*

"I couldn't escape a man who had me by the hair."

"You couldn't?"

"No, but I could do one of two things," she said. "One, I could kill you with my bare hands since you haven't restrained them."

His eyes widened at her words. "Or…" She reached her hand to his head and pulled him into a kiss. Before he realized what happened, he kissed her back, igniting a passion in both of them. His arms wrapped around her, holding her tight. She wrapped her arms around his neck, deepening the kiss. His body reacted in an unfamiliar way, but he enjoyed it.

She finally pulled back for air. "You did say, a guy like you, right?"

"I guess I did."

"So, what happens now?" she asked.

He closed his eyes momentarily. He just crossed a line he shouldn't have. He had warned others not to do this. He had never been tempted himself because he had never had to deal with human emotions. This was all new to him.

"I lose my powers," he said, slowly releasing her.

"What?" She touched her hand to her mouth. "Because I kissed you?"

"I don't think you were the only one kissing here tonight."

"What do you mean?"

"I crossed the line. I should never have let that happen."

"Well, like you said, it takes two. And besides, the alternative was much worse, don't you think?"

"Alternative?"

"Yes. I could've killed you with my bare hands, but kissing you seemed more enjoyable."

"You wouldn't have killed me."

"How do you know that? Can you see into the future?"

"Yes, I can."

11

S he slid down the wall and onto the floor. "So, what will happen with the Vazquez brothers?"

"I can't tell you that."

"Why not? What was it you said earlier? Trust me? I'm trusting you to tell me the truth."

He dropped onto the end of the bed and ran his hand through his hair. What was he thinking? He knew better than to let these physical emotions affect him. Isn't that what he trained his warriors to remember? Being human was much more difficult than he imagined.

He glanced at her. "I will never lie to you, Romero."

"Okay, I think you can call me Elena now, since we... since we are pretending to be husband and wife."

He stood and helped her off the floor, then pulled her into his arms. "This is all new to me." He enjoyed her nearness.

"Really? Because you kissed like you knew what you were doing." She ran her hands across his shoulders then stopped her hands close to his neck. "What powers were you talking about?"

"Teleportation for one." He closed his eyes and thought

himself in spirit form. He glanced at his arms but he could see them. "I guess I lost the ability to transform into spirit form as well."

She touched his face with her hands. "That's not so bad. I can't do that either." He half smiled at her gesture.

"It's not just that. I don't know if I can protect you the way that I should."

"You know, we humans can only do so much as it is. We just don't give up." She pulled his face to hers, into another kiss.

He reciprocated, but this kiss grew even hotter than the last and he wanted more.

His kiss was intoxicating, making her want him more than any man she'd ever known. What was she thinking? She was on a case. She was only supposed to pretend she was married to him. And he wasn't a man, he was an angel. A compromised angel. And she tempted him. *Oh, God.* She pulled away.

"Will I go to hell for tempting you?" she asked.

He leaned his forehead against hers. "No. It takes two to tempt somcone."

"Can you still see into the future?"

He closed his eyes. "Yes, but not far. Free will has a lot to do with it."

"What do you mean?" She backed away, trying to keep temptation at bay.

"I can see the near future, but it can be changed by free will of the parties I'm looking at. Circumstances that change can also change what I see, but I need to touch the person whose future I want to see."

"And the Vazquez brothers?"

"As they pertain to you, I could see that, but we have to be sure they are on this ship first."

"You're right. We need to check out the ship and see if they are on it. At least we know Rodriguez is here. He's creepy." She grabbed her camera bag and unzipped it, trying to put her thoughts of Cummings out of her mind. When she opened it, her camera was not inside. She dumped the contents on the bed. She looked at a cheap, instamatic camera and a small camcorder. She had a Cannon and an extra lens. But something more valuable fell out on top of the foam bottom. Two shiny, golden idols. The kind someone would kill for.

"Is that what I think it is?" he asked.

"Yep." Her heart pounded. They were in deep trouble. "At least now we know they are both here. But how did you get this bag? It looks just like mine." She turned to face him. He was in deep thought.

"A woman was beside me when I handed my ticket to the purser. She was in a hurry, and I thought she had picked up your bag."

"Can you remember what she looked like?"

"Yes. She smelled like a heavy smoker, too."

She picked up the camera and examined it. It was newer and had a card in it. She popped it out. Then she looked at the camcorder. "Nothing on this device. Let's see if they can make prints of what's on here," she said, holding up the card.

"Great idea!" He smiled.

She returned the golden idols to their hiding place, but Cummings stopped her.

"Let me see the backs of these," he said.

She remembered the necklace that was stolen and pulled the two idols back out. On the back of the smaller idol was a slot to attach it to a necklace.

"The woman who took your bag had way too much makeup on and wore a gold chain around her neck."

She went to the brown envelope she had brought with her and pulled out the image of the necklace, handing it to him.

Cummings' eyes widened as he glanced at the image. "Yes, this is what she wore." He pointed to the picture.

"Do you think we have more accomplices?" she asked.

"I'm not sure. Let's get this card printed and find out." He set the image on the night stand. She grabbed her small bag and tossed the room key inside and held the image card in her hand.

"What should I call you?" she asked. She wanted to get more intimate, but this wasn't the time. "If we're pretending to be husband and wife, you call me Elena. What should I call you?"

"Pete."

"Not St. Peter of the pearly gates?"

"Ah, no. Peter never leaves heaven. I'm just Pete, an angel of God." He bowed.

She put her arm through his. "Okay, honey, uh, Pete. Let's go."

They headed to the Atlantic Deck, where the shops were located. Straight ahead was the purser's information desk. The shore excursion office was off to the side of the information desk.

"Here," she pointed. Let's try this one first. She guided Pete through the shop and made her way to the register.

"Do you print pictures from image cards?"

"No, sorry. But the shop on the other side of the elevator does."

She pulled Pete toward the door. "Come on, honey, let's check out that other shop." She pointed across the way.

"You're enjoying this, aren't you?"

She couldn't help beaming as she glanced up at him. He was smiling, too.

Once inside the shop, she noticed a rack of colorful scarves. She loved scarves. She usually wore one in her hair or around her neck, depending on the outfit. She took the image card and handed it to the salesclerk.

"It will be about an hour," the clerk said.

"Great, we'll be back to pick them up." When she turned around, Pete was gone. Her heart pounded. Where was he? He was easy to spot with his Stetson on and he was tall, but he was nowhere in sight. She stepped outside the door of the shop and there he was.

"You scared me."

"I did?"

"I couldn't find you."

"I've got you something." He handed her a small bag.

"Thank you." She opened the bag and found a gorgeous violet/pink scarf inside. "How did you—"

"Lia told me you had a fondness for scarves."

She reached up on her toes and kissed his cheek. "I love it."

She quickly put it in her hair, covering the other scarf. "What do you think?"

"Gorgeous. And the scarf looks good, too."

He reached for her hand and they walked around the Atlantic Deck, waiting for the images to be printed.

When they arrived on the outside deck, she realized the sun was about to set. "I wish I had my camera." Then she remembered her phone. She pulled it out. "Here." She handed it to Pete after setting it for a selfie.

"It's a gorgeous sunset." He held the phone up as they stood close together and smiled. She checked to make sure it came out before putting her phone up.

"My name and address were in my camera bag!"

He glanced down at her.

"They can find us. All they have to do is ask the purser."

"Would they give a stranger our room number?"

"I hope not. But maybe we can find out about them? I've got my badge with me."

"Let's wait until we see the pictures," he said.

They headed back to the shop and picked up the images. "Let's find a place to sit and look at these pictures," she said.

"Over here." Pete led her to a bar. He ordered a couple drinks and an appetizer.

"I was getting hungry," she said. "Did we eat lunch today?"

"I don't remember eating anything but the breakfast you cooked for me."

She pulled out the images and set them on the bar. There were eight total. "This looks like Enrique Vazquez without a mustache," she said. She reached for the appetizer and took a bite.

"This one looks like the woman who picked up your camera bag," Pete said, pointing to the woman who looked like a hooker. "She was wearing the same outfit."

There was another woman with the hooker in a third picture. She wore a gray, long-sleeved dress. A fourth image had Ernesto Vazquez standing with the woman in gray. A fifth image showed the two brothers dressed casually, and both clean shaven. Another two images showed the brothers together in suits, but in one image, Enrique had a mustache and the other, he didn't. The last image was a duplicate of the hooker.

She took a sip of her drink as her stomach growled.

"These pictures definitely show a connection," Pete said.

"I wonder why all four of them weren't posed together."
She glanced at Pete.

"Maybe one of them was the photographer?" He
shrugged.

"Wouldn't they have had three people in the picture if that
was the case?" she asked.

"That's a good question."

"Look at this one, Pete." She pointed to the one of
Ernesto standing with the woman in gray. The woman wore
black oxfords that tied and dark stockings. "This whole outfit
and shoes are something my abuela would wear, but not a
young woman like this. It doesn't make sense." She handed
him the image and picked up the one of the hooker.

This image had the woman wearing heels that looked
more like wedges. Something was odd about the shoes. The
wedge-shaped bottoms were slightly different on each heel.

12

"There's something I haven't told you, Pete." She leaned close to him.

"What is it?" His brows were raised.

"That night, when Tanner was shot, I went after the perp. He hit me across the face and knocked me down. I lost my gun."

Pete ran his hand across her arm.

"I was frantic and felt along the ground for my Glock. When I felt something, I hung on. It was his shoe and he moved. I kept hanging on, but I noticed that one shoe was at least two inches higher than the other."

"And?"

"He wore corrective shoes!"

She pointed to the image of the hooker. "Those are not normal shoes. And neither are these." She picked up the image of Ernesto with the woman in gray. "A young woman would not wear something like this."

He gazed into her eyes. "I love the way your mind works."

"It's all in the details, Pete."

He smiled. A beautiful smile. And she was hooked. Why did he have to be an angel? Why couldn't he just be human?

"Could we have another?" Pete asked the bartender.

The bartender returned with two drinks and set them down.

She pulled out her phone to check her messages and there was one from the captain. She opened it.

Pete took a sip of his drink, then stopped when he saw her face.

"What is it?" He set his drink down.

"Tanner died." Her heart sank as she set her phone down. The tears flowed uncontrollably. She wiped at her eyes, but it was no good.

Pete handed her a napkin and she soaked it in minutes. "Why did this happen?"

Pete stood and pulled her into his arms. He softly rubbed her back, but the loss of her partner would not leave her thoughts. Even with his faults, she still liked Tanner. He wasn't much older than she was. She patted her nose and reached for another napkin.

"Let's go back to the room," he said. He reached for her hand and she held on. He had a strong hand, but she realized he had been gentle. Even when he healed her face. She kept dabbing at her nose and eyes.

"The pictures!" she said.

"I've got them." He raised his other hand. In it was her phone, purse strap, and the packet of photos.

Once inside the room, she headed for the bathroom to wash her face. She checked her reflection in the mirror. Her eyes were still red. She had brought some makeup with her, but barely wore any while working.

Pete knocked on the door. "You've got another text from the captain," he said.

She came out and he handed her the phone. She read the message to Pete. "He wants us to stop the investigation."

"Why?"

She texted the captain back then waited for his response.

When it came, it wasn't what she expected. "He says to just ID the suspects and let the FBI finish the investigation."

"Is that normal for your department?" he asked.

"I don't understand why he sent us on this trip if he didn't want us to finish the investigation."

"Are we in international waters yet?"

"I don't know. But if we were, then the FBI would normally take over."

"But?"

"We've done all the work up to now. I don't know who Taggert is, if he's with the FBI or if there is another agent. I say, we continue our work and let them make themselves known. Then, we can turn over what information we have."

"Sounds good to me."

She checked her phone for the time. "We need to get ready for dinner. You can use the bathroom first," she said.

While Pete was in the bathroom, she pulled out her evening dress and shoes. She looked through the scarves she brought and picked one out to wear around her neck.

She put up the picture Pete had left out on the night stand and put the other photos back in her suitcase to keep safe. Then she returned the image card to the camera and left the camera in the bag.

When he came out, he had on the dress pants and dress shirt he had manifested earlier.

"Hmmm. Nice."

He raised an eyebrow.

She rushed into the bathroom with her things and hurried

through her shower. Luckily, she brought a shower cap to keep from having wet hair.

She put on a minimum of makeup and twisted her hair up into a soft bun, holding it with some hair pins. When she stepped out, Pete was wearing his jacket but fumbling with his tie.

"Wow, you get prettier the longer I know you," he said.

"Thank you. Uh, do you need help with that tie?"

"Does it look like it?" He looked down at the tie.

"It's a little cockeyed." She untied the tie and straightened it before tying it correctly. "I used to help my dad with his tie all the time. He was a cop for over twenty years."

"Really?"

She could feel his breath on the top of her head. "My mother was a dispatcher for the police department. That's how they met."

She looked up into his eyes. They were so close. "You look awesome," she said.

He wrapped his arms around her. "I could say the same about you. How are you feeling right now?"

"I'm okay. As long as I can keep my mind on other things, I think I'll be fine. But just in case, I've got some tissues in my purse."

"Good thinking."

They headed out the door and down the hall. They took the stairs to get to the elevators.

"I didn't think this through," she said. She hiked up her dress to move up the stairs. Being on the bottom of the ship had some disadvantages that didn't matter until she wore a slim-fitting dress. They finally made it to the dining hall and found some seats at a long table.

People began introducing themselves around the table. The last person was Mike Taggert and then it was her turn.

"I'm Elena Romero Cummings and this is my husband, Pete Cummings." She actually liked the sound of that.

"How long have you two been married?" an older man asked.

"We just got married," Pete said.

"Oh? We've been married fifty years. We're celebrating our anniversary."

"Congratulations!" she said. She hoped no one asked any personal questions.

"Don't you wear a ring?" one woman asked her.

She glanced at her bare ring finger. She forgot about a ring. "I, uh, must have left it in the room when I showered this evening.

"I think you put it in your purse," Pete said in a low voice.

She pulled open the purse and found a wedding band and a gorgeous diamond ring beside it.

"Oh, you were right, honey." She pulled them out and put them both on. Then showed them off to the older couple.

She reached under the table and squeezed Pete's leg, then leaned into him and whispered. "I owe you one."

Instead, he took her hand from under the table and pulled it to his lips and kissed it.

When she got a better look at Mike Taggert, she realized she had seen him before. Maybe when she turned in her ticket? In any case, he looked familiar.

There were several courses to the meal and when they finished, she and Pete strolled around the ship, enjoying the stars and each other's company.

He held her hand and they leaned against the railing, looking out at the stars.

"That man, Mike Taggert, was with the purser taking tickets when we boarded," he said.

"I thought so. He looked familiar to me."

"Well, he's been following us around the ship."

"Are you sure?"

"Yes."

"Do you really think he's with the FBI?"

"That's what his Guardian Angel said earlier, and we don't lie."

"Let's head back to the room and see if he follows that far," she said.

When they got back to the stairwell, she hiked up her dress and followed Pete down the stairs. He reached his hand out to her when she reached the bottom.

"Nice legs."

"What?" She dropped her dress.

"You have nice legs," he said.

"Thanks. I exercise. A lot. You never know when you have to chase someone."

He put her hand through his and walked back to their room. When they reached the room, Mike was already in the hall. She pulled out her key and Mike called out to them.

"Hello there."

13

"Mike Taggert. I'm with the FBI." He flipped out his badge."Can I have a word with you two?"

"Sure. Come in." Pete held the door open for Taggert after she got inside.

"I had to be sure you were my contacts. You are with the Miami-Dade Police Department?" Taggert asked.

"Yes." She pulled out her badge and showed it to Taggert. Then Pete did the same.

"I need to go over some things with you about this case," he began. He handed her his card with his phone number.

"What can we help you with?" she asked. She glanced at the card, then tucked it into her purse. She sat next to Pete on the bed after pulling out the desk chair for Taggert.

"You know they found the body of the missing janitor, right?"

"Yes," Pete said.

"Well, they also found the murder weapon."

"What was it?" she asked. She remembered he had been cut up.

"It was a machete with fingerprints belonging to Enrique Vazquez."

"That makes sense," Pete said.

"Oh, we have some other information that may be helpful," she said. She opened the closet and pulled out her suitcase. Inside, she pulled out the envelope with all the images.

She found the note Pete had given her earlier and handed it to Taggert.

"That's information about Garza. He lives in Puerto Rico and owns Fidelity Insurance Company, which insured the Mayan necklace from the jewelry store as well as the two golden idols."

"That's interesting," Taggert said. He glanced over the paper.

"There's more," she said.

Taggert looked up.

"On the night of the jewelry store robbery, we received a tip with the specific information about when and where. Everything panned out, just as the woman said it would, but the call was made from a phone booth in Puerto Rico."

"Puerto Rico?"

"Yes." Pete reached for the camera bag and unzipped it.

"Another thing about Garza was his wife was raped and left for dead a few years ago. The rapist was Enrique Vazquez."

She handed Taggert the rap sheet.

"You two have done a lot of work here." Taggert said, looking at both of them.

"Remember that woman who boarded when I did? She was dressed in pink. Wore a white wig?" Pete asked.

"The one who looked like a hooker?"

"That's the one. She picked up my camera bag by mistake." Pete said. He stood and dumped the contents on the bed, letting the idols fall out. She stood up as well, as Taggert reached for the idols. He studied both items.

"Gloria Escobar." Taggert said.

"Gloria?" she asked.

"Yes, that's the woman's name. Does she know you have this?"

"Once she opens my bag, she will. I had a Cannon camera and an extra lens. My name and address were both inside, along with my phone number."

"Good. Pack everything back up the way you found it and leave it in the room." He tossed the idol back to Pete. "We'll set up surveillance in the hall and monitor your room."

"Our room?" she asked, feeling her privacy was being invaded. Now she knew how others felt.

"Yes. Most likely, she will come looking for it."

"What about her room?"

"We will try to put a bug in her room, too. We've got one in Rodriguez' room already. He's on a different level than Escobar. If nothing else, we'll see about putting a surveillance camera in the hall near her room. This is an older ship, due to retire, so I'm not sure if we can pull off the surveillance, but we're working on it."

"Did you see either of the Vazquez brothers?" she asked.

"No, and I checked everyone. Up to now, we believed they passed this stuff off onto Rodriguez. But now, it looks like it's Escobar."

"We have more," she handed him the envelope of pictures.

She was anxious to see his reaction. He took his time studying the images.

"Where did you get these?"

She glanced up at Pete. "We took the card out of the

camera and had the pictures printed, then slipped the card back inside it." Pete ran his hand over her back.

"I don't get the connection except they knew Escobar." Taggert said.

"Did you see any of these other three on board?" Pete asked.

"No. Do you mind if I borrow these? I need to show my associates so we know who we're looking for."

"Go ahead," she said.

Taggert tucked the photos back into the envelope, along with all the evidence they had gathered.

"I'll bring these back in the morning and meet you here about 11 a.m."

Pete walked Taggert to the door. She picked up the contents of the camera bag and put everything back the way it was. When she finished, Pete stood beside her.

"What do you say we go dancing?"

"Dancing? Do angels dance?"

"How hard can it be? I can learn by watching others."

"I don't know about that. I haven't danced in years."

"Angels are smart and we are fast learners. I've only been human for a day and a half and I've already figured out how to eat, pee, and act like a detective."

She burst out laughing. "You're on."

They headed out to the Atlantic Deck. She had to hike up her dress again to go up the stairs. "This is getting old," she said.

"Not to me. I'm enjoying this very much."

"Of course you are."

They checked out a place where they got a table. The music was good, with a salsa beat. They watched some of the other dancers while waiting for their drinks. Once the drinks arrived, Pete took a sip.

"There's something wrong with my drink."

"Let me taste it." She took a sip. "That's because there's rum in it. She tasted her own drink. "Yep. Rum and soda."

"Did I order that?" Pete asked.

"Apparently, they thought you did. Does alcohol affect angels?"

"I don't know. I've never had alcohol."

"Well, then, tonight we find out." She took another sip. She knew how she felt after two drinks, so that was her limit.

"How about this dance?"

"Sure, why not?" She stood up. She tried mimicking some of the other dancers. After a minute or so, she and Pete got into a groove where it looked like they knew what they were doing. When the music ended, he walked her to the table.

"I'll be right back," he whispered.

She sat there, nursing her drink and listening to the music. Suddenly, she got a cold, prickly feeling. She turned around and behind her was Enrique Vazquez without a mustache. Startled, she spilled her drink. Her hands shook while she wiped up the mess with her napkin.

"Hey doll, how about a dance?" His accent was heavy. A cold chill ran down her spine as he undressed her with his eyes.

"Uh, no thank you. I'm with someone."

"Really?" He leaned close, one hand on the table, the other on her chair. "I see no one here with you."

She fiddled with a loose curl beside her ear. "I said, I'm with someone." She glared at him until he looked away.

"It's your loss, doll. Sooner or later, you *will* be alone. I'll catch you then." He glared at her with dead eyes and no expression on his face. Pete's words came back to her. Evil.

When he finally left, she gulped down the last of her

drink and picked up Pete's glass. She was almost finished with his drink when he returned.

"Where have you been?"

"The men's room," he said, slipping into his seat.

She gulped down the last bit of drink. "We have to leave."

"Now? We just got here."

She stood up and felt light-headed after drinking so fast.

"Right now." She reached over and pulled Pete to his feet. She wrapped her arm through his and led him out the door. By the time they got to the elevators, the 'cold prickly' feeling returned. Tightly holding onto Pete, she glanced around but didn't see Vazquez anywhere. When they finally made it to the stairwell, she slipped off her shoes and hiked up her dress.

"Get your key out," she whispered loudly.

"Are you going to tell me what's wrong?"

"We are being followed."

"Are you sure?"

"Trust me." She quickly descended the stairs. When she reached the bottom step, she shouted, "Run!"

14

She ran hard and fast, clutching her dress on either side, but Pete was beside her. He unlocked the door and they slipped inside.

Pete reached for the lights, but she grabbed his arm and held it away from the light switch. Someone was running down the hall, the footsteps paused in front of their door. She held her breath. Then they were gone.

Pete scrambled across the room to the bed and turned on the light. Still leaning against the door, she let herself slide to the floor on her butt and clutched her chest.

"Now will you tell me what's going on?" He came to help her off the floor.

"When I finish with my seizure, I will." She breathed hard and still felt light-headed. Pete pulled her to her feet then wrapped his arms around her. He stroked her back, running his fingers lightly over her shoulders. It helped her relax. She could feel the tension slowly leaving her body. He kissed the top of her head.

"Are you okay?"

"Not yet." She took a couple of deep breaths. She had let

Enrique get to her. But it was fear she felt. That was something new for her. She usually had more confidence in her abilities, but this was altogether different.

"Who was following us?" Pete asked.

"Enrique Vazquez." She exhaled loudly, then pulled away slightly to look into his eyes. She hadn't realized how brown they were until now. She almost forgot what she was saying. "While you were in the men's room, Vazquez asked me to dance. When I refused, he threatened me."

His brows furrowed and he ran a hand through his hair. "I should never have left you."

"Pete, I've never felt so vulnerable as I did then. Usually, I have my gun and I feel safe. But tonight…" She shook her head.

He pulled her close and tightened his arms around her. She felt safe and she held on, reaching her arms up his back. She wanted to stay this way.

Can I keep him, Lord?

She felt him harden against her. He lifted her chin and covered her mouth with his. She kissed him back and let him deepen the kiss. His arms reached lower down her back, so she put her arms around his neck. She felt him lift her off the ground. She wanted this to continue when she realized they stood beside the bed. He lowered her to the ground, and she fumbled with his buttons.

"Here, let me," he said. He closed his eyes momentarily and they both stood naked in front of each other.

"Now that's a cool power." She beamed at the sight of his magnificent body.

He scooped her up and set her on the bed. He continued kissing her mouth and moved to her neck.

"Oh my." The sensations from his touch sent heat

throughout her body. "I'm all yours, Pete." Her voice came out raspy.

"This is all new to me," he said. He kissed her throat and moved down to her breasts.

"You're doing a great job so far. And if either of us screws up, the other won't even know, right?"

He stopped and smiled at her, then continued moving down her body.

He continued exploring her body in ways she never imagined, with pleasure building with each passing minute. She wanted this moment to continue, but when he stopped, she explored his body. She kissed, licked, and caressed him all over. She wanted more, but he stopped her, and they finally came together in heated passion.

When they finished, she squeezed him to her with her arms and legs wrapped around him. *I'm keeping you for myself.*

"I'm keeping *you* for *myself*," he said. He pushed up to face her.

"Did you just hear my thoughts?" she asked.

"Loud and clear." He rolled over and pulled her on top of him. He moved a curl from around her eyes.

"I like when you do that." She pushed herself up to look into his eyes.

"I like the way you smell, the curls that hug your face, the way your skin feels." He ran his hand slowly up and down her arm. "I like the way you kiss, the way you touch me, and the way you taste," he said.

"I like everything about you," she said. She bent her head and kissed his chest. "But I especially love the way you made love to me."

He turned on his side, pulling her with him, then kissed her tenderly.

She wrapped an arm and a leg over him and closed her eyes.

Thank you, Lord.

The next thing she knew, there was a loud, blaring noise beside the bed.

Pete stopped the noise then turned to her.

"Come on, let's go see the sunrise." He smacked her bare bottom.

"Hey!" She was half asleep when he rolled out of the bed. He grabbed some clothes from the drawer and headed into the bathroom.

She found some clothes and headed there as well.

"Move over, Sweetie," she said as she stepped into the small space.

"Not much room in here, is there?" He shampooed his hair.

"Well, it's more fun this way," she said. She squeezed some shampoo into her hand and washed her hair.

They took turns rinsing off and hurriedly dressed.

"You aren't going to dry your hair?" he asked.

"It will take too long. Besides, it'll be dry when we're done."

Both clad in shorts and t-shirts, she grabbed her purse and phone and headed out the door behind Pete.

"I'll be glad when I get my camera back," she said. They climbed the stairs and headed to the elevators.

"Is it me, or does the ship feel like it's rocking just a little?" she asked.

"I feel it, too. The seas are getting rough," Pete said.

They got to the outside rail just in time to see the light show. She started taking pictures. She grabbed Pete and moved him over to get him in the shot. The clouds were dusted with a beautiful dark-pink glow, hanging in a dusky sky.

"Here, my arms are longer," Pete said. He took her phone and pulled her next to him with the sunrise behind them to their right. He got a few pictures and showed them to her.

She kissed him on the cheek and he snapped another one, showing it to her.

"I love it," she said.

"You know, a beautiful sky like this comes with a warning."

"What do you mean?"

"Sailors have a saying, 'Red sky at night, sailors delight. Red sky in morning, sailors take warning.'"

"What does that mean?"

He kissed her cheek and squeezed her tight. "It means there's a storm brewing. You know that hurricane we heard about on the news?"

She vaguely remembered the reports and nodded.

"We're heading right for it."

That's all they needed now to complicate things. Things were already complicated with an angel she had compromised, two criminals on the loose, and these new feelings she had to deal with.

"What do you say we go work out before breakfast?" Pete asked.

"You're on!" She poked him in the chest.

They headed to the Caribbean Deck and found the gym. No one else was there this early, so they each started out on different pieces of equipment.

"You know, after last night, I feel as if I need to do some gymnastic work to keep up with you," she said.

"Is that a bad thing?"

"No. I didn't know angels were so…versatile."

"So you're saying I wasn't bad for my first time?"

"That was my first time, too, so I have nothing to compare it with."

"Okay, so we're both playing it by ear, then."

"I guess you could say that."

After her workout on the treadmill, she moved over to weights, while Pete continued his treadmill workout.

She pulled down on the weights when she heard a familiar voice behind her.

"Hello, doll."

She froze. Glancing over her shoulder, there stood Enrique Vazquez in a Hawaiian, floral print shirt, white pants, and shoes. She would not let her fear get to her. His type fed off fear.

"I told you I would catch you alone."

"But I'm not alone." She stood to face him.

"Really? There's no one here but you."

15

She quickly scanned the room. Where was Pete?

"I'm with someone. I'm not interested in you so you may as well leave."

He made a move toward her and she jumped into ready position, her hands near her face. The one advantage she had was her police training.

He took a swing at her, but she blocked with her left arm. He took another swing and she blocked with the right arm. She rocked back on her left foot and kicked high with her right foot, connecting with his face. He fell backward, landing on his butt. *Pete, where are you?*

Pete came around the corner. Enrique scrambled to his feet and was out the door before Pete caught up to him.

Adrenaline pumped through her veins.

He touched her shoulder. "Are you all right?"

"I've got to run this off." She headed to the treadmill and flipped on the machine. She was at a full run in less than a minute. "Adrenaline rush," she said.

"I went looking for a water fountain," he said. "I didn't even leave the room and he still managed to terrorize you."

"Pete, I'm okay. I'm not mad at you, I'm just pumped up. I've got to work this off." She had not experienced a rush like this in years. It took her another thirty minutes of running before she felt calm enough to quit.

"Come on, I'll show you where the water fountain is." He led her around the corner of the room and she drank deeply.

"Now, I'm hungry," she said.

Pete led her to their room to change for breakfast. When they got there, she realized her hair was wet with sweat and her clothes smelled. She grabbed a sundress and some panties.

"I'm going to need another shower," she said.

Pete pulled her into a kiss. "Hmmm. I think I'll join you," he whispered. "Get the water ready."

She winked and headed into the bathroom.

Pete sat on the bed and moved the camera bag out of the way while he pulled off his shoes. He couldn't wait to jump in the shower with Elena. The thought of the water dripping over her naked body excited him. He stood and pulled off his wet shirt when he heard a knock on the door.

"Yes?" He opened the door. No one was out there but a laundry cart full of dirty linens. He glanced down the hall in both directions, but saw nothing. He turned to go inside, when an arm came from behind him, covering his mouth with a white cloth.

Elena hung up her clothes and got the water ready. Then she peeled off her sweaty shorts and t-shirt and stepped into the shower. She wet her hair and applied shampoo again. After lathering her hair and rinsing it, she realized Pete was still not in the bathroom. Maybe he changed his mind. It was a very small shower and he was a big guy. The thought of his naked body made her smile. She finished dressing and wrapped a towel around her head and stepped out of the bathroom.

"Pete, I—"

Pete was not in the room and the camera bag was gone.

16

Why would Pete—she stopped short when she saw Pete's shoes and socks on the floor, next to his wet t-shirt. She gasped at the thought that something happened to him. She had to find Taggert. She checked her phone. It was almost 9:00 a.m. It would be another two hours before Taggert showed up and she had no idea where he was staying. She slipped on a pair of shoes and struggled with her zipper. She grabbed her purse and key and checked the contents. Nothing was missing.

She hurried to the stairs. She noticed a door beneath the steps that she hadn't seen before. She had been preoccupied before with Pete, and hadn't noticed it. Across from the door was a service elevator.

She climbed the steps up to the Atlantic Deck, bypassing the elevators altogether. The purser was at the desk and didn't appear to be busy.

"Hi! I need to know what room Gloria Escobar is staying in, as well as Juan Rodriguez."

"I'm sorry, I can't give you that information. Privacy, you know."

"Yes, that's what I thought. Could I get a message to Mike Taggert, then?" She needed help.

He quickly glanced down his list of passengers. "We don't have a Mike Taggert listed. Could he be staying with someone else?"

"That's possible. Could I speak to the captain? It's urgent." Someone had to help her find Pete.

"I'll see." He picked up the phone and dialed the Captain's Office. He spoke in low volume where she couldn't hear what he said. "He said you could see him now, if you'd like. He's on the bridge. Would you like me to show you where that is?"

"Yes, please." She tried not to panic. People don't disappear off cruise ships every day. Do they?

The purser walked her out onto the deck and gave her directions to the Boat Deck, where the bridge was located.

She found her way to the bridge and stepped inside.

"Captain?"

"Yes, may I help you?" *I hope so.*

She walked up to him and spoke softly so as not to alert the others as to what she was about to say.

"You have an FBI agent, Mike Taggert, on board. It's imperative that I see him right away. My partner has disappeared and I'm afraid something has happened to him."

"Come with me, Miss…?"

"Romero. Elena Romero. I'm traveling with my partner, as Mrs. Pete Cummings. Did Taggert brief you on anything?"

"Very little, I'm afraid. He said it was a 'need to know' basis." He held the door for her. She stepped into an office.

"What exactly has he told you?" she asked.

"There is an investigation going on about a robbery suspect. That's all he told me."

"Do you know where Taggert is staying?"

"Yes. He and two other agents are sharing a room in the staff's quarters on the Twilight Deck, room 27. But you can only get there with a key to the service elevator."

"What is the room that is directly across from the service elevator, under the stairs on that Deck?"

"Oh, that's a storage room. There is one on every floor by the stairwell. You'll need a different key for that room as well."

"Can I use your phone to call Taggert?"

"Let me do that for you. I'll have him meet you here."

The captain did as he said while she looked around his office. He had credentials on the walls, along with a few portraits of himself and the main staff.

"Agent Taggert said he would be right up. You can wait here if you like. I need to be on the bridge. We have a hurricane to deal with." He shook her hand and left.

Hurricane? So Pete was right. The ship did feel like it was moving faster as well. Not that she doubted Pete, but she didn't want to think about a hurricane with all that had happened.

She paced back and forth in the small office. She had to figure out what to do. Was Lia trying to talk to her? She felt compelled to look in that storage room. And did Taggert and his men get those cameras into position? Maybe Taggert had more news for her. She thought of all the clues she and Pete had spoken about to see if there was anything she missed.

Taggert walked into the room. "What is it? What's wrong?" he asked.

"I was hoping you could answer that question for me. Did you get those cameras hooked up?"

"No. We had no way to hook up a feed for the video with such short notice."

She wrung her hands. "Pete's missing and so is the camera." She let out a breath she didn't know she held.

"Are you sure he didn't try to return it on his own?"

"Yes, positive." The fact that he was barefoot and shirtless in a pair of shorts, and stood her up in the shower, was proof enough for her.

"Come with me." He held the door for her. "We know that Juan Rodriguez was in his room when the captain called me. Escobar had left her room, but we were unable to follow her."

"We've got to find Pete, Agent Taggert. His life could be in danger."

"Call me Mike, please. And why do you think that?"

"The fact that he's missing tells me that they know he is a police officer, or he can identify them."

"Yes, but you and I can also identify them." Taggert's watched beeped. "Excuse me." He tapped an ear piece and then spoke into his watch.

"We're going to check Escobar's room first. She was spotted on the Horizon Deck."

She and Mike took the service elevator and reached the Caribbean Deck in a few seconds. The doors on this elevator opened on either side. One side faced the interior of the ship and was used by staff only. The other side faced the exterior of the ship. When they arrived on the deck, Mike checked with his colleagues.

"Let's go. She's still on the Horizon Deck." He pulled out his set of master keys, and opened Escobar's room. He entered first, pulling out a small handgun from an inside holster.

"How did you—?"

"Shhh!" He put a finger over his lips.

No one appeared in the room. Mike motioned he would check the bathroom, and she checked the closet. She didn't think Pete was here. Her gut feelings centered on that storage room by the stairs.

Inside the closet was something interesting, however. Besides a gray dress, there was a man's suit and a pair of black oxfords, and two men's dress shirts. She checked the drawers. There were shorts and t-shirts, men's socks and underwear.

Mike came out of the bathroom.

"Any signs of Pete?"

"No. How about you?"

"Nothing here. Let's go."

As they stepped out of the room, Mike got another beep on his watch.

"Rodriguez' room is clear. We'll check it as well."

"Yes." She wanted to look for clues in there as well.

As they rode the service elevator back to the Atlantic Deck, she had a thought.

"What was Escobar wearing?" she asked Mike.

He looked puzzled, then called through his watch and listened through his ear piece. "She's wearing a pink dress."

The elevator opened. The two of them went to Rodriguez' room. Mike went in first, checking everything out. Then, she went in and checked the closet, while Mike checked the bathroom.

The men's clothes in the closet caught her eye. Especially the Hawaiian floral shirt and white chinos. There was a pair of white running shoes. Inside one of them was a thick wedge. When she opened the drawer, she saw her camera bag on top. She opened it. Inside was her camera and lens and her name and address.

"Let's go. There's nothing here."

"Nothing?" She just found a treasure trove. She slipped the camera bag over her shoulder and headed out with Mike.

"Did you have that going in there?" He pointed to the camera bag.

"No, but it's my camera and I'm taking it."

Mike furrowed his brows.

"They took their camera bag back and I'm taking mine. Now, let's go check out that storage room."

"That's not how it's done. They have to return it. We can't let them think we've been here."

"At this point, I don't care what they think. They are criminals and I'm taking back my camera."

Mike shook his head and followed her down the hall.

"If you've got this room bugged, did Rodriguez say anything about Pete?" she asked.

"He doesn't talk to himself, much, so no. But he did have a visitor."

"Male or female?"

"Male, why?"

"What did they talk about?"

"Eating mostly. And they talked about what shows to see, but that was last night."

"Do you suppose they know the room is bugged?" she asked.

"I hope not. They certainly didn't act like it."

Mike unlocked the service elevator. She stepped inside.

"Why are we checking this particular storage room?" he asked.

"My Guardian Angel told me to," she said, glancing up to heaven. "I have found when I listen to her, the right things happen."

"Oh yeah?"

"You should try it. It may save your life one day."

He raised his brows at that.

"Tell me, Mike, when will you be arresting Escobar and Rodriguez?"

"We've got to catch them with the idols in their possession. And since Escobar didn't have the camera bag until now, we can arrest her when she carries it, but we don't have any hard evidence on Rodriguez."

"Can't you search both of them?"

"We have no evidence. Unlike you, we can't go on hunches."

The elevator stopped. She walked over to the storage room and listened, while Mike unlocked the door. She thought she heard a muffled sound and her heart pounded.

"Pete? Are you there?"

There it was. A definite muffled sound. She pushed against the door, but something blocked it. Mike tried with no luck.

"Wait a minute." She turned sideways and wedged herself between the door and the door facing. Her heart still pounding, she popped through to the other side. There was a laundry cart blocking the door, caught between some shelves and the door. She closed the door and pulled the cart toward her. It was heavy. Two bare feet shot up over the edge.

"Pete! Oh, God!" His feet were bound together with plastic straps the police use for extra handcuffs.

Mike wedged himself into the room.

"Have you got a pocket knife?"

He pulled one out and cut the band off Pete's legs, then he cut through his hand restraints. When Pete turned around, he cut the restraints that held the towel in his mouth.

"I hope that was a clean towel!" Pete said. He spit out the lint from the towel.

"Are you all right?" She helped him out of the cart.

He grabbed her shoulders. "Do you know how long I've been in that cart?"

"Yes! I've been looking for you the whole time."

"She had a hunch you'd be in this storage room," Mike said.

"A hunch?" Pete asked.

"Lia told me."

"Thanks, Lia," Pete said as he glanced over her shoulder.

"Who's Lia?" Mike asked.

"Her Guardian Angel." Pete said.

"Let's get him back to the room, and I'll fill you in on what we've discovered since we saw you." She gave him a squeeze.

"Where are we, anyway?"

"The Twilight Deck," Mike said.

"You mean, I've been here all this time? Just down the hall from our room?" He glanced at her.

"Lia showed me this room right away, but I had no way to get in here. It took me a while to get to Mike and then here. They have the camera bag, but I found mine."

"Where did you find it?" Pete asked.

"In Rodriguez' room," she said.

"Rodriguez? It was Escobar who took it."

She unlocked their door and the three of them went inside.

"Why don't you shower, Pete, while I fill Mike in on what we discovered."

. . .

He raised an eyebrow. Since when did Agent Taggert become Mike? It was almost two days before she called him Pete. He grabbed some clothes from the drawer and headed to the bathroom.

He didn't know if he liked that. And why was he feeling this way? He wanted to hug Elena after his ordeal and he couldn't because Mike was there. If only he hadn't answered the door. Then again, whoever knocked him out could have entered while they were both in the shower and possibly injured them.

But they only used chloroform to knock him out. They wanted him out of the way and not dead. But since they took the camera bag, why didn't they trade her bag in exchange? And the fact that they only took the bag while she was in the shower could mean they didn't know she was there.

After filling Mike in on what happened to her on the dance floor and in the gym, she hesitated to tell him about the shoes. She had told her captain in the past that she had hunches a lot of the times, but now she knew it was Lia telling her things.

"Be sure to examine those photos of the Vazquez brothers more closely. I'm sure you'll find more clues if you do," she said.

"I will. I'll check back on you two tonight in case you learn anything more," he said.

"Thanks." She walked him to the door and then locked it after he left.

"I don't think he's ready for me to tell him about my hunch, Lia. At least, not yet. He didn't even want to believe you told me where to find Pete."

She leaned against the bathroom door and knocked before peeking inside. "Want some company?"

"You're too late," he said. He zipped up his jeans and tensed his jaw.

"Too late? What do you mean? You're the one who stood me up. What happened?"

"I had planned on joining you when someone knocked on the door."

"Really? Who was it?"

"No one. Just a laundry cart. But when I turned around to come inside, someone grabbed me from behind, covering my mouth with a chloroform-soaked cloth. I don't remember anything after that."

She moved close to him, touching his chest. His voice was unemotional to say the least. He tried to pull a shirt over his head, but she caressed his chest and kissed him there.

"Don't," he said. He finished pulling his shirt down.

"I thought you liked that."

"I did." He tried to move past her, but she stood in his way. She crossed her arms under her breasts.

"Okay. What is it? I know something is bothering you and I'm not moving until you tell me what it is."

He tensed his jaw. But she held his stare.

"How long have you and Mike been on a first name basis?"

"Mike? You mean, Agent Taggert?"

"That's exactly who I mean."

"He asked me to call him Mike after I called him Agent Taggert all morning. It sounded so formal."

"Yes, and Mike is very informal, almost personal." He crossed his arms over his chest.

"I recall," she stepped closer to him, "that you refused to

call me Elena or even Romero the first day. You kept calling me Detective, remember?"

He did remember. He didn't want to get personal and thought she had an attitude. But here was Taggert, getting personal right away, and he didn't like it. Besides, that was before he got to know her. Before he was attracted to her.

"That was before I...that was different. You're my partner."

She ran her fingers across his chest, tracing an imaginary line. "Do I sense a little jealousy here? Because that's not an angelic trait."

"No." He tried to ignore the stirring in his loins from her touch.

"I had to have his help in locating you, Pete, in case you're wondering why I even called him. He has a set of master keys."

He kept his stance, arms crossed, legs apart, staring at the wall and not looking at her. He wanted to stay mad at her, but she made sense.

"Besides, his eyes aren't as sexy as yours. His muscles aren't as large as yours, and...I'm not the least bit interested in him. He's not even an angel."

He grabbed her wrist and pulled her closer, wrapping his arms around her. "Are you sure?" He touched her forehead with his.

"Positive," she breathed against his lips. He brushed her lips with his, then deepened the kiss. She reciprocated, pulling him closer to her until his stomach growled.

She pulled away slightly, patting his belly.

"That reminds me, Pete, this is the last seating for lunch. If you're hungry, we better go now or we'll have to find some other place that's serving food."

He growled. "I'm starving." He turned her toward the door.

His hand caught the zipper part of her dress. "Did you know you were unzipped?"

"Yes. I wanted you to help me with it earlier, but you weren't here. I think it's stuck."

He tried to pull it up, but it was caught in the fabric. He couldn't get it to budge. "I'm afraid you'll have to wear this dress for the rest of your life," he teased.

"Well," she ran her fingers across his chest. "If you are really nice to me, I'll let you blink it off me later like you did last night."

"You promise?"

"I promise."

"Let's go eat."

She grabbed her new scarf and purse. While she wrapped the scarf around her, he took her camera and shot some images of her. The scarf covered the zipper problem. He slipped the camera over his shoulder.

They found their seats in the dining room. It looked like some of the same people were eating with them from last night.

"So what did you tell Taggert while I was showering?" he asked.

"I just told him about what happened last night and in the gym."

"So, what took you so long in finding me?"

"Taggert insisted we look through Rodriguez' room and later Escobar's room." She drank some of her tea.

"Find anything interesting?" He dug into his Chicken Kiev.

"I did, but I don't know if Taggert saw it." She tore her bread in half, taking a bite.

"And what was that?" He took a bite of his vegetables.

"Besides the ugly gray dress in Escobar's closet, all the other clothes were men's clothes."

"Men's clothes? I saw her wearing a pink dress yesterday."

"Yes, and she wore it again today. No woman would wear the same dress two days in a row if she was going to be in the same place both days." She took a bite of her chicken.

He cocked his head and narrowed his brows.

She looked right at him. "No woman." She took another bite of her chicken.

"And what about Rodriguez?"

"He has the same taste in clothes as Enrique. He even has the same foot problem, too."

"Someone must have paid them to steal the idols," he said. He finished his vegetables.

"I think so, too. I just don't know where this Ramsey fits in," she said.

"Maybe it's an alias or someone they have to meet in Puerto Rico," he said. He took a drink of his tea.

"I think we should be there when they leave the ship and follow them," she said. She finished her vegetables.

"You know the FBI will be there, too. And they won't let us arrest them. It's not our jurisdiction, remember?"

"Yes, and remember they didn't see either Vazquez brother board the ship."

"What do you mean?"

"Pete, I don't think they are picking up on the same clues as we are. Besides, I told them everything we know and discovered. If they don't figure things out for themselves, I sure as hell am not going to tell them." She wiped her mouth with her napkin. "How about a walk around the deck?"

"Sure." He helped her with her chair.

She pulled out her phone. "We need to apprise the captain of what we've found out." She tapped her phone.

"What's wrong?"

"No phone service. We must be in international waters. I guess I'll have to try again later." She put her phone back in her purse.

"Well, from here on out, we stick together. No more running off and meeting up with each other. You are not leaving my side. You got that?" He pointed his finger at her.

"Yes, partner. Got it." She saluted him. She glanced out the porthole glass.

It was pouring rain outside.

"So much for swimming today," she said.

"The water is getting rougher, too. But if you want to swim, I'm pretty sure there's an indoor pool here, somewhere."

"Let's see if we can find a map and see where it is," she said.

They got to the Atlantic Deck and picked up a map.

"We'll have to go back to the room to change first," he said. "But I want you to do something for me."

"What's that?"

"Put on the Armor of God."

"Like in Ephesians?" she asked.

"Yes. We're fighting a spiritual battle and since I can't change into the spirit, we both need our armor. Lia can do only so much. And it wouldn't hurt for you to ask for a legion of angels to help us battle these evil spirits surrounding the Vazquez brothers."

"Okay. No problem. Let's take the stairs," she said.

He saw her make the sign of the cross, and heard her prayer. *Lord, I pray for a legion of angels to surround me and Pete. And I put on the armor of God, in Jesus' name I pray.*

. . .

They were on the Caribbean Deck, going down, with Elena first and him right behind her. Elena stopped, then backed up into him. When he looked over her shoulder, there stood Enrique Vazquez.

He backed up the stairs, holding onto Elena, until he felt something sharp in his back. He turned to face Ernesto Vazquez, with his back to Elena.

"Hello, doll. You have something of mine," Enrique said.

"I have nothing of yours," she said.

"I want the camera bag you took from my room."

"That's my camera bag," she said.

"Not anymore." Enrique flipped open a switchblade knife and touched it to Elena's chest.

18

"Today, we finish this." Enrique said.

Elena held her breath when Enrique slid the knife under her new scarf. He pulled up, cutting the scarf in two. She watched it fall down her arms and float to the spiral stairs below.

"Damn you," she said. She tightened her fists. That was the scarf Pete bought for her. She wanted to deck him for that.

Pete reached his arm out between her and Enrique and pulled her up to his step.

"Keep your hands off her," he shouted.

"Move it," Enrique motioned with his knife.

Ernesto backed up, allowing Pete and her to follow him. Ernesto reeked of cigarettes.

As they stepped into the hallway, there was no one in sight. Ernesto unlocked the storage room door and forced Pete into the room at knife point. The storage room was small and similar to the one Pete had been put in earlier. There were shelves across the three walls with linens, towels and pillows. Ernesto pushed her into the room as well. Both Vazquez brothers stepped inside the cramped space.

"I want the camera bag," Enrique said.

She saw Pete shift something on his shoulder. *Her camera.*

"It's in the room on the bed." He pulled out his key and tossed it to Enrique. Enrique caught the key in his knife hand, and used his other hand to punch her in the face, knocking her into the shelves. She rubbed her jaw, the familiar pain from the night on the street coming back to her.

Pete grabbed Enrique and threw him against the wall by the door, while she jumped out of Pete's way.

"Touch her again and I'll kill you."

Ernesto picked up a metal bucket, but before she could yell, he hit Pete in the back of the head with it. Pete fell to the ground, dazed, landing on her camera. *Ouch!*

Ernesto quickly fastened some plastic restraints on Pete's feet. And before Pete could turn over, Ernesto had Pete's hands behind his back, using the same kind of plastic restraints on his hands.

Enrique pulled her up by the hair, and twisted her arm behind her back. She managed to escape his grip on her arm, but she couldn't get away from his grip on her hair.

Ernesto dove for her feet while Enrique grabbed both her arms, releasing her hair. She kicked and wiggled, trying to free herself, but they were both persistent. Ernesto managed to restrain her feet while Enrique restrained her wrists. Two against one was definitely not fair.

Pete struggled to get up, but Ernesto kicked him hard in the gut and then pushed down on his back with his foot. She heard a cracking sound. *Was that his ribs or her camera?*

Enrique pulled his knife out and drew a "V" across her chest while holding her hair.

"Just a little souvenir to remind you of our time together, doll." He grinned with an evil look in his eyes. "If we meet again, I'm afraid you won't live to regret it. But for me, it will be quite memorable. Adios." He pulled her close and kissed her hard, then shoved her down on her butt.

"Bastard!"

Ernesto and Enrique locked the two of them inside the storage room.

"Pete! Pete, wake up!" He wasn't responding. She would have to figure a way out herself. She glanced down at her bleeding chest and noticed her purse strap. It took several minutes of struggling before she could get the strap in her mouth. She drew her legs up to hold the purse in her lap. Then she struggled to open the purse with her teeth. All she had were nail clippers, but that would have to work. They were attached to her key chain. She worked for several minutes, trying to drop the key chain over her shoulder and into her hands. Once she got the key chain in her hands, she worked several minutes trying to cut through the plastic restraints, but the plastic was too thick.

"What are you doing?"

She jumped at the sound of Pete's voice and dropped the keys. "See what you made me do! I was trying to escape."

"Would you like me to help?" he asked.

"Uh, yeah."

He blinked his eyes and the restraints fell off.

"Why didn't you do that sooner?" she asked, rubbing her sore wrists.

"I was unconscious."

"Okay. Fair enough."

He pulled her into his arms. "I've never been so mad before. Threatening to kill someone is not angelic behavior."

"No, it's human behavior. And believe me, Pete. Right now I feel the same way about those two. How are your ribs? I heard something crack."

"Yes. I healed myself and your camera. I got the worst of it. He pulled away, lifting up her chin. "Hold still while I heal you."

She did as he said, gazing into his eyes. He looked so determined as he touched her lip with his fingers. Then he used both hands against her chest. This time, he closed his eyes momentarily. When she looked down, the 'V' was gone, along with the blood.

She touched her face. "My jaw definitely feels better. Thank you."

He kissed her sweetly on the lips. "Yes, everything works just fine."

"Why do you suppose they want the camera bag?" she asked.

"Did it have an interior pocket?"

"Yes."

"Did you check it when you found it?"

"No."

"Maybe they hid the gold chain in there."

"Ah. Good thinking. Let's get out of here," she said.

Pete put his hand on the knob but it wouldn't turn. "It's locked from the outside. There's a deadbolt, too."

"Can you blink us out of here?"

He closed his eyes, holding her hand. When he opened them, they were still inside the closet.

"It didn't work," she said.

"That would have been shape shifting, so I guess that's out completely. And we know teleportation doesn't work anymore."

"Hey, but you can still heal and blink my clothes off."

He smiled. "Thanks for the encouragement."

"It's better than any human trait I can think of."

"Well, you're good at solving puzzles, Elena. And God

put me here for a reason. If you hadn't prayed for a legion of angels to help us, we wouldn't be here now."

"Did you see the future?"

"Yes. There were so many evil spirits surrounding the brothers that Enrique would have finished us off. Lia couldn't fight them all herself. With the legion fighting, they kept the evil spirits busy so that Enrique and Ernesto forgot their original plan."

"Is that how it works?"

"Sometimes."

She looked up to heaven. "Thank you, God!"

"So now, we wait."

They sat on the floor together. She leaned against Pete's arm.

"I was just thinking about what you said, Pete."

"Oh?"

"You were mad enough to kill someone."

"To kill Enrique, you mean?"

"Yes. I bet Mr. Garza was just as mad when he found his wife butchered by him."

"But Enrique was caught and sent to prison," Pete said.

"Yes, but he got out. If I were Garza, that would piss me off. I would want revenge. I would still want Enrique dead."

He glanced at her. "Those are strong emotions."

"That's what I'm getting at, Pete. They are strong, human emotions. What if Garza set this whole thing up?"

"What are you talking about?"

"We both thought someone paid the Vazquez brothers to steal the golden idols, remember?"

"Yes?"

"What if Garza paid them to steal the idols so they would get caught?"

19

"**D**o you think Garza wants the idols for himself?" Pete asked.

"If it were me, and Enrique had hurt you like that, I'd set him up and then kill him. I'd make it look like an accident or self defense."

He pulled away and studied her. "I hope you're thinking like a criminal."

"No. I'm thinking like a man who is embittered that the system let a criminal out who is a menace to society. A criminal who should remain in prison for life. A man who loves his wife so deeply that he would do something like that. A man who would take matters into his own hands," Elena said.

He let all that process in his mind. Human emotions were starting to make sense the longer he remained human. But from a spiritual standpoint, they didn't.

"Not to change the subject, but do you think the ship is moving faster?" she asked.

"It is. I can feel it."

"Can you feel the rocking, too?"

"Yes. I'm starting to wish we hadn't eaten."

"Seasickness," she said.

"Will it go away?"

"I sure hope so."

"We may be trying to outrun the hurricane," he said.

"Can you see ahead? Are we heading back to Miami?"

"I'm not sure if we're heading back to Miami, but I see us in a jungle, chasing the Vazquez brothers." He put his arm around her and pulled her close. He didn't like this queasy feeling in his gut but he couldn't change back to spirit form to avoid it. How did humans put up with this roller coaster of emotions? He wasn't completely powerless, but he had to adjust his thinking. He had to focus on his strength and his ability to see ahead. He knew Taggert was looking for them. It was only a matter of time.

There was a noise at the door. Muffled at first, then louder. It sounded like voices. Elena pulled away and stood up.

"Did you hear that?"

He stood. He knew it was Taggert. He had seen it.

She pounded on the door. "Help! We're in here."

The knob jiggled. The deadbolt moved. When the door opened, Taggert was on the other side.

"Thank goodness!" Elena said.

"Are you two all right?" Taggert asked.

"Yes, but it could have been worse," she said.

"What took you so long?" Pete asked.

"Well, I didn't know you were missing until I found Elena's scarf on the ground. And even so, I didn't realize you were in danger until I discovered it had been cut with a very sharp knife."

"Makes you wonder how they got those knives on board?" Elena asked, her arms crossed in front of her.

"I believe they sell them in the gift shop," Taggert said.

"Well, that would have been handy to know," she responded sarcastically.

Pete put his hand on her back as they stepped out of their small prison.

"Any injuries?" Taggert asked.

"Yes, but Pete took care of it." She walked past Taggert.

"What?" Taggert glanced at both of them.

"It's a long story."

"Well, there's been a change in plans," Taggert said.

"How so?" he asked.

"We're docking in Puerto Rico in about an hour." Taggert glanced at his watch. "Then, we're pulling out and heading west."

"Hurricane?" Pete asked.

"Yes. We're unloading passengers with one-way tickets. The remainder will stay on board as we head to another island to wait out the storm."

"Any new developments in the case?" she asked Taggert. They stopped in front of their room.

"No. I'm heading to the Horizon Deck to watch for the Vazquez brothers." He shook hands with her, then Pete. "Take care of yourselves."

She pulled her key out and opened the door.

There, on the bed, was the camera bag, upside down. Elena headed to the bed to inspect the bag.

"Well, whatever it was, it's gone. The only things in here are my lens, lens cloths, and a few batteries."

She opened a drawer. "Do we have time for a shower?" She pulled out some jeans and a t-shirt.

"I'd love to take you up on that shower, but I'm afraid we'll miss the Vazquez brothers," he said. He leaned against the wall, watching her.

"You're right. If we don't go out there, Taggert will miss both of them. He's looking for the wrong people."

"Are you thinking what I'll thinking?" he asked.

"I'm not sure, but I'm going with my gut feeling, Pete. Help me with this dress." She turned her back to him and pulled her hair out of the way.

He realized the zipper was still stuck, so he blinked her clothes off. He couldn't resist and smacked her butt.

"Whoa! I really love that power." She quickly dressed in her jeans and t-shirt.

He changed clothes as well and put on some running shoes Elena made him manifest earlier.

He checked her camera while she put on her running shoes as well.

"The camera seems to be working just fine. I managed to get a few good shots of you earlier," he said.

"I hope I was dressed!"

"Of course."

She grabbed her purse and the two headed out the door.

He grabbed her hand and they worked their way to the Horizon deck.

The place was packed with people huddled under a sea of umbrellas. The boat rocked more as the ship docked.

"I can't see a thing," she complained.

"Of course not." He squeezed her shoulders. "You're too short."

"Oh, I suppose you can?"

"Not really. Too many umbrellas."

The view of San Juan was obscured by the heavy rain.

"You know, my father was born here," Elena said.

"Really?"

"Yes, but it's the first time I've been here. Do you see Taggert anywhere?"

"No."

The ramp lowered and the boat lurched a little in the rough water. Someone bumped into Elena and him from behind when that happened, but Elena lost her balance and fell. He leaned over and helped her up, grabbing her around the waist.

"Pete!"

He touched her lips with his finger. He knew what she saw and tried to stop her from blurting it out. There wasn't much time now. The crowd pushed forward down the ramp. He held onto her hand, and kept his eye on the targets.

When the two entered the cab, he made note of the number and he grabbed the next cab. He opened the door and pushed Elena inside. They were both soaked.

"Follow that cab!"

20

The cab driver took off, following the other cab.

"Did you see what I saw?" she asked Pete.

"Yes. I got some great shots of the two of them."

"When I fell, I knew it was them. I saw Enrique's shoes. He was wearing the black oxfords. And I could smell Ernesto's cigarettes."

"I could smell him, too."

He ran a hand through his hair. "I wish I had my hat."

She touched his unshaven cheek. "I like that hat on you."

He took her hand and held it in his, lacing his fingers through hers.

"Do you think Taggert figured it out?" she asked.

"Well, if he didn't, he's not good at his job."

She turned and glanced out the rear window. No one followed them. She only hoped Taggert would figure it out in time. She had given him enough clues, but her hunches she kept to herself. She pulled out her phone and his card and texted him. 'We're following the brothers in a cab. Hurry.' She tucked the items back into her purse. Neither of them had weapons and they were going up against a very dangerous man.

The driver turned up the radio. Salsa music played.

"This reminds me of our dance the other night." She patted his hand. If only it had lasted longer.

He smiled.

An announcer burst into the music with a message in Spanish. The driver slowed the car. "Huracan! Huracan!" he said.

"No! Follow that cab," she shouted. She leaned forward, pointing ahead.

The driver shook his head.

She pulled a twenty out of her purse and threw it at the driver. "Pronto!"

The driver took off once more, mumbling under his breath. The other cab was further up the road, the tail lights a small red blur. She glanced around and realized they drove through a very wooded area.

"What was that about?" Pete whispered.

"The hurricane is heading this way. He didn't want to go any further," she whispered back.

"I guess money talks in any language," he whispered.

The rain got heavier. The road disappeared into a gray blur. The driver sat close to the steering wheel, his hands pumping up and down, trying to keep the car on the road. The car hydroplaned, and the wind blew them sideways.

"Madre de Dios!" he shouted, crossing himself in prayer. He tried to straighten the car, but the wind whipped him around. She was thrown around in the back seat, even with her seatbelt on.

"I think we're turning," Pete whispered.

"Mira alli!" The driver pointed to the red tail light in the distance.

"Yes." Pete nodded.

"No! Huracan! You go now." He motioned to the door.

"That's our cue," Pete said. He manifested some money and threw it at the driver. He opened his door and pulled her outside with him, in the pouring rain.

The water was below Pete's knees in the road way, but higher for her. They walked through a path, wading in the dirty water. On either side of the watery path was a tropical jungle.

The rain stung her face, like pellets. They had to find the brothers and hold them with the evidence until the FBI or authorities showed up. Other than that, they had no jurisdiction here and no weapons.

"God help us," she mumbled.

He glanced at her. "We can use another legion of angels once we get there."

"Send us a legion of angels, Lord. We need all the help we can get." Then she remembered Enrique's warning that she would not live to regret their next encounter. "And I'm putting on your armor, Lord."

Suddenly, two headlights came toward them.

"We've got to get to higher ground," Pete shouted. He lifted her up toward some bushes on the side of the road. She scrambled to get her footing. Once she felt sure, she reached out a hand to Pete.

Pete couldn't get his footing and slipped back down the side of the road.

The lights got closer.

"Give me your hand," she shouted.

Pete tried again. This time, she pulled with both hands as hard as she could and Pete managed to get his footing. The two of them fell over in the bushes.

"I underestimated your strength," he said. He pushed up off her.

She propped herself up on her elbows, water dripping down her face. "Yeah, well, don't let it happen again." She poked him in the chest.

He helped her up. "Remind me to properly thank you later, when this is over."

"You can count on it." She winked. "Now, let's go."

When the cab went by, she noticed only the driver was inside. At least now she knew the Vazquez brothers were up ahead.

He took her hand and the two of them made their way toward a shed near a large tree.

"Wait here and I'll see if they are inside." Pete said.

She wrapped her arms around the tree to keep from being blown away. She was too cold to argue with Pete now. She wanted more than anything to get to a warm, dry place. Every muscle in her body was tense from trying to stay warm. She fought off hypothermia.

Up ahead, she could see Pete crouch low and move toward a window of the shed. She saw him peer through the window. He took pictures of what was inside.

Suddenly, a gust of wind blew the roof off the building. It flew through the air, hitting the tree she clung to. She pulled her arms away the moment the roof left the shed. The four walls fell down in four different directions. She saw the two brothers scatter out of the shed and she could see Pete's head under one of the wooden walls. She remained behind her tree and waited.

"You all right?" She heard Pete's voice and peered around the edge of the tree. She glanced up over the piece of tin roofing that clung to the tree.

She nodded and ran toward him and wrapped her arms around him.

"You're trembling," he said. He kissed her head. "We've got to follow them. Come on."

She clenched her teeth from the cold and moved with Pete through the jungle. They waded through the water again, keeping the brothers in sight. Up ahead was a building. A home, maybe? But whose home?

They hid behind some bushes and watched the two brothers make a move toward the house. The gusting wind tried to separate her from Pete, but she held onto him and he had her tight against his body.

One of the brothers was tossed backward with another gust of wind. He recovered and joined the other at the door. Then someone opened the door, but the two pushed their way inside.

Pete glanced at her. "Who was that?"

"Kleinman."

"Come on. Let's find a back entrance." He pulled her with him as he ran to the right of the front door. All the windows were boarded up, so there was no way their movements could be detected unless there were security cameras.

They came around the back side of the house and there was a door. The wind was much stronger on this side of the house. Pete slowly turned the knob and pulled but nothing happened. He straddled the door with his feet on either side and tried again, making a small opening. She squeezed between the door and the door frame. Pete pulled as hard as he could but couldn't open the door wide enough for himself. She found herself inside a laundry room. She braced herself against the door and walked backward, pushing as hard as she could to open the door for Pete. He squeezed inside and the two of them slowly walked the door in until it closed without slamming.

Pete opened the dryer and found a couple towels. He handed one to her and they both dried off as best they could. She wrapped herself up in the towel and removed her shoes. Pete had done the same and she placed them on the top of the dryer and then covered them with her towel.

She moved to the interior door and listened first, then slowly opened it a crack. She heard voices but they were muted.

Pete was behind her, looking over her shoulder. She pulled the door further and peered out into the hallway. Her heart pounding from her recent ordeal. To the far left was another door. The front of the house, maybe? To the right was a kitchen with a bar separating it from an open dining area. But diagonally in front of her was another door.

Before Pete could stop her, she moved across the hall and opened the door. She stepped inside a dark room. Pete caught the door and moved in behind her. The small room contained shelves with various sizes of cans and boxes. *Must be a pantry.*

The voices grew louder.

"…get the money now or no deal." It sounded like Enrique.

A cold chill ran through her as she shuddered, remembering his last words.

"If you had waited at the hotel, like you were supposed to, I would have brought you the money."

That one sounded like Kleinman.

"Vamos, 'Rique." It was Ernesto. He sounded like he was pleading with his brother.

Then she heard the familiar sound of a switchblade being opened, like the one he used on her.

"'Rique, no! Hombre!"

Then a gunshot went off, piercing the silence and something in the pantry. Her heart skipped a beat as she heard a grunt from Pete.

Oh, God! No! She moved her hands in the air, feeling for his body, but couldn't locate him anywhere. She heard a scuffle in the next room. She bent down, feeling along the floor until she found Pete. There was something warm on the back of his head.

Oh, please, God! Please let him be all right. She felt for a pulse. *Thank you, God!* He was alive and breathing. There was something large and round near his head. A can. A can with a bullet hole in it. Something was pouring out. She smelled it. *Tomato sauce?* She shook her head. He must have been knocked out when the can hit him.

Suddenly, a light came on from the floor. *A trap door?* A woman held the light on herself and then on Pete. She opened the door wider and reached for Pete's legs. She pulled him toward the hole.

Elena picked up Pete under the arms and followed. He weighed a ton. Together, they got him down some steps to a basement. There was an air mattress on the floor and they set Pete on it.

The woman quickly went back and closed the opening, while Elena quickly inspected Pete for injuries. When the woman returned, she shined a light on Pete. Tomato sauce covered his head and he had a knot on the back of it from where the can hit him. He appeared all right except he was unconscious.

"Mi nombre es Carmela Garza, y tu?" she whispered.

"Elena Romero," she whispered and pointed to herself. "Usted habla ingles?"

"Yes, I speak English."

"Great. My Spanish is rusty. Is this your home?"

"Yes, it is."

"This is my partner, Pete Cummings. We are police detectives for the City of Miami and we are after Enrique and Ernesto Vazquez for the robbery of the Metro Museum and a jewelry store in Miami."

"Aye, Dios mio! If only you had arrested them at the store."

"Was that you who called me?"

"Si, yes. I wanted you to capture him. Arrest him."

"Actually, I arrested his accomplice. He escaped from my partner after shooting him. My partner later died."

Carmela pointed at Pete.

"Pete is my new partner."

"You are in great danger. You must leave."

"I…we can't leave. There's a hurricane out there. Do you want to tell me what's going on?"

Carmela got up and went to a small kitchenette and picked up some wipes and returned with them. Then Carmela knelt beside Pete and started wiping the tomato sauce from his hair and handed her a few cloths. She wiped Pete's face. *God, please keep Pete safe.*

"Carlos wanted to set a trap for Enrique Vazquez to steal the idols so he could be caught and arrested. He wanted him back in prison for life after what he did to me." Carmela lowered her head. A tear fell from her face. "I can never have children, thanks to that monster."

"Where is Carlos?"

"When he heard Mr. Ramsey was having trouble getting them to leave, he decided that he would make it look like they broke into the house. He took the gun and went upstairs. He said not to come up there, no matter what."

"No one knows you are here?" she asked.

"Only Carlos."

"How did you know I was in the pantry?"

"I heard your footsteps. I knew you were on the other side of the room. I didn't know who you were at the time, but I heard him fall after the gun shot. I thought someone was hurt."

"I need to check on Mr…uh…Ramsey, as well as your husband. All I have to do is hold the Vazquez brothers until the police or FBI show up."

"How do you plan to do that? You are alone, yes?"

"Have you got any rope?"

"Yes." Carmela went to a drawer and pulled out some clothesline cord and handed it to her.

"What about a gun or a knife?"

"Carlos has the gun."

She glanced at Pete, touching his cheek. She wanted to stay and nurse him back to health, but she had a job to do. No one was safe until she captured Enrique.

"What about a pocket knife? Any knife?"

Carmela went back to the kitchenette and came back with a paring knife.

"This is better than nothing." She took the rope and cut it into four pieces. If only she knew the art of lassoing a steer. It might come in handy tonight.

She patted Pete on the cheek. "Take care of him for me, Carmela." She stood up and headed for the pantry opening. Carmela followed her to lock up behind her.

"I'll knock on the floor three times so you'll know it's me, okay?"

"Be careful, por favor," Carmela pleaded with her hands in prayer.

"I will." She stepped into the pantry and waited for her eyes to adjust to the darkness. She could hear some voices again. It was the two brothers, talking about food. Then she heard footsteps coming toward the pantry. She moved to where she could be hidden when the door opened, but she put her hand on a large can, just in case. All she had was the element of surprise and she had to do it right the first time. She tried to remember how tall Ernesto was, and raised her hands above her head.

21

The door opened slowly. The light went on and caused pain in her eyes. She could see his outline and came down hard on his head. He fell to the ground. She pushed the door closed and worked fast with two of the ropes. She managed to tie him up good before he moaned. She hit him again with the can and he went limp. She checked his pulse. He was still alive, but something hung around his neck.

She tapped on the floor three times. Carmela opened it with a flashlight shining on the floor. She helped her with Ernesto, bringing him down the stairs. They left him on the floor against a wall. Then she noticed it. He wore the gold necklace that was taken from the jewelry store. Attached to the bottom was one of the golden idols. She let him wear the gold pieces as a reminder of why he was now tied up. She then fastened the ropes so his hands and feet were tied together.

Carmela ran to the kitchenette and came back with a towel and some duck tape. She shoved the towel into his mouth, while Carmela taped it in.

"That's going to hurt when it's removed, but he deserves it," she said. "This way, he can't walk, talk, or run. You'll be safe."

"This is not Enrique," Carmela said.

"I know. This is his brother, Ernesto. He'll have a headache when he wakes up." Hopefully, he would remain asleep for a while.

She moved back to the pantry. Carmela fixed the floor entrance once she was inside the pantry.

Enrique was a totally different matter. She found the paring knife where she left it and gathered her other two ropes.

A strange feeling came over her. *Is that you, Lia? Is our legion of angels here?* She felt a 'yes' whispered in her ear.

She left the safety of the small pantry and headed to the dining room across the way. She listened for sounds or voices, but didn't hear anything. She moved around a corner of the wall. There was a small sitting area at the far end of the dining room. In one of the seats was Kleinman, with a knife sticking out of his chest where his heart used to beat. Behind him was a bookshelf. The bullet must have gone through that wall and penetrated the pantry. But where was Carlos? Where was the gun? And where was Enrique?

Pete moaned and opened his eyes. What happened? And… where was he? He was lying on some type of bedding. How did he get here? He rolled over and saw Ernesto slumped against a far wall. He sat up. His head ached. He touched the back of his head and found a large knot. *The things humans do to themselves was astounding.*

"Oh, good. You're awake." A woman came up to him.

"Who are you? Where am I?"

"I am Carmela Garza. You are in my basement. Your partner went upstairs to get Enrique Vazquez and help my husband, Carlos."

"Elena?" He touched the knot on the back of his head and prayed. It was healed immediately. *Thank you, God, for my healing.*

He stood up. "How did he get here?" He pointed to Ernesto.

"Your partner knocked him out. I helped her get him down here. He's tied up at the moment."

"How do I get up there?" *He had to be there. This is why he was sent. Why did Elena go up there alone?*

"Come with me," Carmela said.

They went across the basement to the other side. She showed him a trap door in the ceiling, just above a set of stairs.

"When you come out," she whispered, "you'll be in the closet. Turn left and you'll be in the entryway. The living room is farther left from there."

"Thanks, Carmela," he whispered back. He had to find Elena. Why did she try to take on Enrique alone? They were partners. They were supposed to work together.

— *That's what I've been trying to teach her. This is a lesson she will learn the hard way.* —

He now realized why he was sent. He had already let Elena down when they were trapped in the storage room and now here.

He climbed the stairs. Her life was in danger and she had no weapon. His gut tightened at the thought of her facing Vazquez again. He better not lay a hand on her. Anger boiled up inside him.

Elena moved across the room as quickly as she could and leaned on the wall, listening for sounds. Her adrenaline pulsing through her body. The lights flickered. She could hear the storm raging outside. She took a chance and peeked around the corner. Carlos was tied and gagged in a Straight-back chair. Enrique was in a chair nearest her, with his back to her. Carlos glanced up at her. She pulled back quickly. She reached for a lamp, yanking the cord out of the wall. Enrique came around the corner. "'Nesto. Donde estas?"

She swung high with the lamp, like a baseball bat, and connected with Enrique's head. He fell back, swearing in Spanish as the lamp broke in two.

She ran to the bookcase, grabbing a statue she had seen, and pulled the knife out of Kleinman's chest, but Enrique recovered quicker than she expected. He grabbed her arm. She broke loose, twisting out of his grasp. She connected the statue with his head with her other arm.

He grabbed her again, but she broke loose again. She kicked him high in the chest with her bare foot. He fell over backwards.

"A woman with an attitude. I like that. I'm going to enjoy taking you."

"The hell you will. I have a legion of angels helping me."

God, send me a legion of angels now! Please! She stood in ready position.

Enrique laughed and dove at her. She jumped aside, barely getting away. She ran toward Carlos and tossed him the knife.

Enrique was up again and grabbed her hair, pulling her back. She put her hands up to her head, the pain was intense.

He had a death grip on her hair. They were in the room with Carlos.

Enrique pulled her toward him and tried to kiss her. She held him off with her forearms against his face.

He took his free arm and pulled one of her arms away. She punched him hard just below the sternum, knocking his breath out of his lungs.

Carlos, in the meantime, had worked the knife against his ropes.

Elena grabbed another lamp and connected with Enrique's head. He shook off the plaster and came after her. She ran into the dining room around the table. Enrique's eyes flashed in anger.

"I'm going to enjoy killing you," he said. He shoved the table into the wall, cornering her. He jumped onto the table and came at her. She squeezed through the opening between the table and the wall and went under the table, trying to escape. She was going to have to kill him because he wouldn't stop until one of them was dead. She ran out from under the table, but he jumped her from above, knocking her down.

He turned her over, pinning her hands down with one of his hands, above her head. He straddled her hips, unsnapping and unzipping her wet jeans.

What was he thinking? Even she had a hard time removing her wet jeans. Her legs were free. She swung her legs high, lifting her hips off the floor. She grabbed him around the neck with her feet and pulled him down hard. He fell off her, but when she turned to get away, he grabbed her pants leg. She kicked at him, but he grabbed both her legs and pulled them out from under her, along with her pants.

He cussed her in Spanish. She heard a commotion in the other room, but she was too busy with Enrique.

Pete finished cutting Carlos free from his ropes. "Go to Carmela, she's worried about you. I'll take care of this."

Carlos looked up at him. "Gracias, senor. Gracias!" Carlos went to the bedroom where the trap door was located.

Pete moved to the dining room where Enrique had Elena's hands over her head, he was straddling her. She was half dressed.

"Let her go, Vazquez!" He ran toward them.

Enrique glanced over his shoulder, but tightened his grip on Elena. She twisted her hands once more, breaking free. Enrique turned to look at her. She straightened her palms and smacked him hard over both ears at the same time. He fell on top of her.

Pete grabbed Enrique off her with both hands and tossed him like a rag doll across the room. Enrique lay still on the floor.

He reached down and helped Elena up off the floor, pulling her into his arms. A loud cracking noise sounded above their heads. He grabbed her jeans off the floor and ran with her into the bedroom as a tree cut through the roof, landing on top of Enrique.

22

E lena slipped on her jeans and knocked three times
on the trap door. Things started blowing around the
house, while rain poured in through the gaping hole
in the roof. Her heart still pounded in her chest.

She descended the stairs with Pete behind her. She
thought about what she had done to Enrique. She never had to
use that defense before. She was told that it would either
make someone violently sick or kill them. It was a shock to
the nervous system. But there was no time to check for a
pulse. His eyes, flashing in anger, would haunt her now. She
shook the thought from her mind. She was cuddled up with
Pete on the floor in Carmela's basement and she was safe.

Ernesto was across the room. He had come to, but
couldn't sit up because of his ropes.

Pete cut the duck tape, holding the towel in his mouth.

"Where's Enrique?" he asked.

"Dead." Pete answered him. He returned to Elena.

"What? You killed my brother?"

She glanced up at Pete. His jaw clenched.

"A tree fell on him," Pete said.

Carmela made the sign of the cross and mumbled a prayer.

"I don't believe you. I heard fighting upstairs," Ernesto said.

"Believe what you want. When this is over, you can see for yourself," Pete said.

He rubbed her shoulders. "Are you cold?" he asked.

"Yes, and overwhelmed." She'd managed to stay focused throughout the ordeal. *Thank you, Lia.* Now that it was over, she couldn't stop shaking. This must be what shock felt like. She was dazed by what had transpired upstairs. How much time had passed since she left this basement? Her jaw clenched and she shook all over. It seemed no matter what Pete did, she couldn't stop shaking.

Carmela left the area and returned with a couple blankets.

"I don't have any clothes for your size, but here are some blankets."

"Thank you," she said. She took the blankets offered, handing one to Pete. He wrapped one around her, then the other around himself. She felt his arms tighten around her and she felt safe. Why did she think she could handle Enrique alone? What was she thinking? Pete was her partner.

If Pete hadn't gotten there when he did, she would be dead, along with Enrique. Her body ached from trying to stay warm, then fighting off Enrique. He was heavy and strong. There was no way she could have gotten his dead weight off her in time. And Pete threw him aside as if he weighed nothing.

Pete ran a hand through his hair. He thought about the events that had just happened.

Why bring me here, Lord, if I didn't make a difference?

– But you did make a difference. –

How? Elena did fine without me. She handled an evil by herself.

– No. She remembered your advice and called for a legion of angels. They kept the evil spirits busy, while she fought Enrique. –

She almost died because I failed her. I failed you, Lord.

– You didn't fail me or her. She learned a valuable lesson. –

What is that, Lord?

– She finally learned that she can't do this alone. She must trust in Me for help. And trust her partner to watch her back. –

I lost my powers. I was useless.

– No. You had everything you needed. I woke you the moment you needed to be awake. It was all part of my plan. You were in the right place at the right moment in time. –

What now, Lord? How do I continue to serve you?

– You have options now that weren't available to you before. Choose wisely. The next step is up to you. –

Elena shivered even though Pete had his arms around her. She didn't know if it was from the cold, wet clothes, or the fact that she killed someone.

It was her first kill. Usually the department would provide counseling in a situation like this and give her time off. She would have been counseled after Tanner was shot, but she was too busy then.

But here she was, in the basement of strangers, somewhere in Puerto Rico. She was in the arms of an angel who lost his powers because she tempted him. And because of the other people around her, she couldn't confide in Pete, her temporary partner.

She had mixed feelings about all this. What would happen to her? What would happen to Pete? She didn't want to lose him, but she was not in charge. God was in charge. He knew what would happen, that's why he sent Pete to help her. She would be dead if it weren't for Pete's actions. He was a partner she could trust. He pulled his weight, even though he was learning on the job.

Carmela and Carlos had been sitting at the table. Carmela got up and filled an enamel coffee pot with water. It was an old camping coffee pot that perked coffee the old-fashioned way, on a propane stove. Her abuela made coffee for her like that when she was younger. She glanced around and realized they used a propane lantern as well. The power was out. Even below ground, she could hear the faint howling of the wind outside. She thanked God she and Pete made it inside before the worst happened.

Carmela wrapped a blanket around Ernesto. "I have no quarrel with you, señor." She went back to the table with Carlos and spoke to him. Carlos moved to a closet and pulled out another air mattress and set it up for him and Carmela.

Pete fixed one of their blankets on the other air mattress, like a pallet.

"Lie down," he said.

She did as he said. He lay next to her and wrapped his arm around her, pulling her close and covering them both with the other blanket.

"Are you all right?" he whispered in her ear. "You're still shivering."

She turned toward him. "I…I'll be all right." But she wasn't sure that was true. Would Pete think less of her now? Would he still want to be her partner? Would God let him stay a human? She couldn't stop shivering.

Pete moved her hair out of her eyes. "Lia told me your deepest thoughts," he whispered.

"She can hear my thoughts?"

"Yes. She told me you were worried."

"I have so much on my mind, I can't relax."

"We're still partners, if that's what you're worrying about. If you'll have me," he whispered.

She reached up and touched his face. "I want that more than anything."

"Good. That's settled. Now maybe you can relax." He kissed her forehead. She clung to him until Carmela brought them some coffee.

She sat up and felt Pete wrap the blanket around her shoulders. Carmela handed both of them a cup of coffee.

She sat, holding the coffee and letting the hot steam warm her face. Pete sat next to her.

"This feels good," she said. Her face warmed up.

"You're supposed to drink it," he teased.

"I know that. I'm just savoring the heat from the cup and the steam. I want to enjoy every bit of this coffee."

She took a sip. Although it was black, it still tasted good and warmed her body from the inside. When she finished, she leaned toward Pete and kissed his cheek. "Thank you for saving my life," she whispered.

"I didn't save your life," he said.

"You most certainly did. That tree landed right where I was lying. I couldn't move. You rescued me."

Pete shook his head. "You saved yourself. I merely helped you to your feet."

She poked his chest. "You and I both know you did more than that. You were in the exact spot I needed you to be, at precisely the right moment. And only God could coordinate something like that."

He took her hand and kissed her fingers. "You're absolutely right."

Ernesto groaned as he leaned against the wall.

"I guess I should loosen his bindings," she said.

"How did he get down here?"

"You were unconscious when Carmela and I brought him down here. But, pretty much the way you did."

"And how did I get down here?"

"When the gun went off, it hit a can in the pantry that hit you in the head. I couldn't find you. I thought you were shot. I…thought I lost you." Her eyes watered at the memory.

"I felt around and thought it was blood coming from your head, but it was tomato sauce. Carmela and I cleaned you up after we got you down here. Then I had to use a large can on Ernesto, but it took two blows to bring him down."

"And your point?

"He has a harder skull than you?"

She walked over to Ernesto and loosened just enough where his feet were no longer tied to his hands, but both were still tied separately.

"Clever. Did you do this?" Pete asked.

"Yes. When I spent summers with my abuelo I learned how to tie up a calf."

Pete helped Ernesto sit up.

"Gracias," Ernesto said.

"Do you want something to drink?" Pete asked him.

"Agua, por favor," he said.

Carmela brought him a plastic cup of water she poured from a milk jug stacked against the wall.

Elena sat near Ernesto. "The police or FBI will interrogate you when this hurricane is over. You know that, don't you?"

He nodded. "Who are you?"

"I'm Detective Elena Romero, and this is my partner, Detective Pete Cummings. We were investigating the two crimes Enrique was involved in before he left Miami. If you want to talk about it, we'll be right here. If you want us to call someone for you, we'll do it when this is over."

"Thank you."

Pete helped her off the floor and they walked back to their side of the room.

Carmela was working on something in the kitchenette. She walked over to Carmela and put her arm around her shoulder.

"Thank you, Carmela. I'm sorry you had to go through this. Is there anything I can help you with?"

Carmela set a pot on the propane stove. "I'm heating up some soup. We may be here awhile. You can set the table." She pointed to a cabinet above her head.

She opened it and found paper plates, bowls, and plastic cups. She took them out and set the small table for four people, since there were four chairs.

Carmela handed her some plastic spoons and napkins, which she set out. She realized she hadn't set a table since she lived at home. When she was at her parents' home, there was always someone to talk to. Dinner was their social time together to exchange thoughts on things, talk about the news, their daily lives. She realized how much she missed that, living alone.

Now, both of her sisters were married with families of their own. She was the only spinster. She went back to where Pete sat and joined him.

He ran his hand around her shoulders. "Are you still cold?"

"I think I'm good now."

Moments later, Carmela announced the food was ready. She took a small tray to Ernesto with soup in a cup, some crackers and a canned drink. Then she joined the other three.

Carlos said grace and they ate their soup in silence.

"Tell me, Carlos, did you see who killed Kleinman?" Elena asked after a long silence.

"Kleinman?" Carmela asked. She glanced at Carlos.

"He went by the name Ramsey. And yes, I did. There was a struggle between Enrique and Ramsey. Enrique stabbed Ramsey in the chest before I could get my gun. I tried to shoot Enrique, but I missed. He tackled me before I could get off another shot. Then the two of them tied me up in the chair," Carlos said.

"You know the police will be questioning you both for your part in this?" she asked.

"Yes, I suppose," Carlos said. There was a sadness in his eyes.

"I would advise you to get a good lawyer."

"I will. I didn't know this was going to happen. I just wanted to set him up with the stolen idols and have him arrested. Ramsey had another agenda. He wanted the idols for himself. I offered money to entice him to steal. I even paid for the cruise tickets. Ramsey was supposed to meet them at a hotel here in San Juan, where he would call the police. He showed up here instead. I certainly wasn't expecting the other two."

"Perhaps Ramsey changed plans without telling you," she said.

"No, don't you remember? They argued about that." Pete said. He caught her gaze. "When we were in the pantry, Kleinman had told them they were supposed to meet him at a hotel."

She remembered that now. She glanced at Ernesto. "Why did you two come here?" she asked him.

"Our cousin was the cab driver. He drove Ramsey here from the hotel. Enrique had him drive us here, instead of the hotel."

The howling wind had diminished. Carmela got up and turned on a portable radio.

"The eye of the hurricane is passing over us. The worst is yet to come," she said.

"We might as well get some sleep. It is late," Carlos said.

Carmela showed her and Pete where the bathroom was. After taking turns, they all found their spots. Carmela and Carlos had pulled a third air mattresses out and set it up. Each couple had their own mattress as well as Ernesto. Once everyone was settled in, Carmela put out the propane lantern.

Pete wrapped his arms around Elena, pulling her close. He had worried about her shaking earlier. He covered her in a warm blanket of air. One more of his gifts he still had. While he lay there beside her, he tried to imagine his life before meeting Elena.

He constantly trained warriors for battle with evil spirits. When he didn't do that, he trained Guardian Angels for duty to a human. They kept humans safe from harm and evil influences. When their humans were attentive, like Lia said Elena was, it was easy to speak to their spirits and warn them of dangers. Some humans didn't listen and got into more trouble.

But Elena didn't need another Guardian Angel. Lia had done her job well. If he went back to duty as an instructor, would he regain his powers? Or were they lost for good? He couldn't change back into spirit form and he had tried a couple times since he and Elena had become intimate. With Tanner gone, Elena did need another partner. She had problems in the past with other partners. Would her captain let them work together since they had been intimate? Is that something her captain needed to know? What did humans do about something like this?

'They get married.' Lia said.

He didn't remember dozing off, but he remembered being awakened by a loud pounding noise above the ceiling. Elena was missing.

He smelled hot coffee and sat up. He glanced around the room. Ernesto sat up. Carmela was pouring coffee and speaking to someone, but it wasn't Carlos. It was Taggert.

But where was Elena?

24

The hurricane must be over. Taggert came to speak to him. He squatted down near the air mattress and looked him over.

"Must have been a hell of a night for you," Taggert said.

"What took you so long?" Pete asked. He ran a hand through his hair. The memories of the last twenty-four hours were still vivid in his mind.

"That's the same thing Romero asked me. We were looking for two men. Obviously, you two stumbled upon them dressed as women. They barely let us off the ship before it took off for safer waters. We had to go over Romero's notes to figure things out. When I got her text, we had to involve the local police."

He watched two local police officers take Ernesto into custody after untying him and cuffing him back.

"Where's Romero?" he asked. He glanced around and didn't see her anywhere.

"She's upstairs overseeing things." Taggert chuckled and shook his head.

Pete saw movement to the far side of the basement. It was

Elena, descending the steps. She approached them, carrying some shoes. "I thought you might like to see this, Taggert," she said. She dropped her shoes, along with Pete's beside Pete, and held up a single shoe.

"Now why would I want to see a man's shoe?" Taggert asked.

"Recognize it, Pete?" She turned it over for him to see it was a corrective shoe.

"Enrique's shoe?" he asked.

She lifted the inner lining, exposing the other golden idol.

"Damn! That's how he did it," Taggert said.

"You did remove the golden idol and chain that Ernesto was wearing, didn't you?" she said.

"What?" Taggert ran back to the opening, where the local police just took Ernesto. "Hey, wait!" he shouted. Taggert climbed the steps in a hurry.

Pete stood up and approached Elena and wrapped his arms around her. He kissed her forehead. "I wonder why they wanted the camera bag."

"Maybe they had the idol in it when I had it," she said.

"Where is your camera?" he asked.

"In the cabinet over there. I forgot to tell Taggert you got some great images of the brothers."

"Well, we will have to write up a report at some point, won't we?" he asked.

"Yes. You're the first partner who remembered that piece of information. Most of them left it to me." She poked him in the chest.

"I'm not like the others, Elena, if you haven't figured that out yet. And I know I have a lot to learn as far as police work goes." He moved some loose hair behind her ear. How could he explain this to her? He actually liked doing this kind of work. There was a satisfaction in capturing and stopping evil.

"So, what happens now?" she asked.

"What do you mean?"

"Well, now that you fulfilled your mission, what happens to you?"

"The Lord said the next step is up to me."

"And? Have you decided?"

"I've been an angel for thousands of years, Elena. Training Guardian Angels and warrior angels is always the same, predictable routine. There's no emotion involved, just the training. But being human is very different. There are so many overwhelming feelings. Even a routine like yours is new and unpredictable every day. There are more variables to consider, like other people's reactions and emotions. Especially with you. I have a feeling that nothing is routine with you."

"Well, you're right about that. I can't do the same old thing every day. I sometimes go with gut feelings, or maybe it's Lia telling me something and then everything changes." She glanced up at heaven. "So, are you trying to say you're interested in remaining my partner?" Her brows rose in hope.

"Only if you'll have me as your partner. I don't want to work with anyone else."

She reached up on her toes and kissed him. "I don't want you working with anyone else, either."

She pulled away slightly. "I need to check in with the captain. He must be frantic." She gave him one last squeeze before releasing him. He enjoyed her touch.

What if he wanted more than that? What if he wanted to be her life partner? What did Lia call it?

Marriage.

⁓

"Captain?"

"Romero? Damn, it's good to hear your voice. I've been worried about you. Is everything okay?"

"Yes and no. My phone is about to die. I'll need some counseling when I get back, sir."

"Why? What happened?"

"I killed Enrique Vazquez, Captain." There was a silence.

"Captain?"

"How?"

"I'll explain later. I'm stuck in Puerto Rico until they get the airport up and running. It's heavily damaged. I won't be able to get back anytime soon."

"What about Cummings? Is he all right?"

"Cummings is fine, Captain. I'll write down what happened and get you some kind of report as soon as I can."

"You do have some time off built up, Romero. Keep me posted."

"Yes, sir."

She watched Pete pull the camera out of the cabinet, then head upstairs. She hurried after him.

A police officer, standing where Enrique had been, wrote things down. They had hauled off the two bodies. Where the living room stood was a huge ficus tree, taking up the entire living room and dining room. It was like the house was cut in half. Each side seemed intact except for the middle. Carlos and Carmela walked off with the police to a waiting cruiser. Another cruiser pulled away with Ernesto in the back.

Taggert approached them.

"We're getting ready to leave if you two need a ride?"

"Where are you heading?" Pete asked.

"We have a hotel room." He handed Pete the business card for the hotel. Pete handed it to her, since he had no phone.

She punched in the number.

"Sorry, we are full." She got another number from the hotel clerk and punched that in. She found the same answer, only this time, the clerk gave a little more information.

"Everyone's full, due to the hurricane, but there are a few shelters that may have room. We need to get our reports done while the information is fresh."

"Okay. We'll take you back to the hotel with us to do that, and then find you a place to stay," Taggert said.

One agent got in the front seat and Taggert and another agent got into the back seat of the police cruiser, with the officer driving. Pete sat next to Taggert in the back and pulled her into his lap.

"This is cozy," she said.

He wrapped his arms around her and she leaned against his chest. She loved the way Pete made her feel safe.

"I'm going to need a phone charger when we get there," she said. Her phone was in the red and would eventually turn off.

"I think we can help you there," Taggert said.

The ride seemed to take forever, but Pete never complained about her weight on his legs. She was afraid to make conversation with Pete, so she kept still. The other three men didn't speak, making the ride almost unbearable. Finally, she had enough of the silence.

"Okay, this is too solemn. It feels like we're going to a funeral," she said.

The ice was broken.

"You're right, Romero. I can't wait until this is over." Taggert said.

"Looks like the hurricane is headed for Miami, Taggert," one of the agents said, glancing at his phone.

"I guess we'll be stuck in paradise for as long as it takes to get a plane off the ground," the third agent said.

"Darn. Stuck in paradise? I don't know how I'll be able to manage it," Pete said, glancing at her. He winked.

The other men laughed. Not her. She smiled.

25

Elena and Pete found a quiet place in the lobby to work on the reports. Taggert got them some paper and pens.

"All you have to do is write down what you remember from start to finish," she said. "The way it happened, from your perspective. All the details you can remember as well, that pertain to the case."

"You mean I can't write what happened between us?" He gestured with his finger, pointing at her and then himself.

"Definitely not!"

He smiled.

"I'm serious. Only what evidence we found pertaining to the case."

He nodded. She had forgotten he had never been a police officer before. Surely he wouldn't put in their intimate moments together. "I'll read your report when you finish and you read mine, okay?" That would ensure he didn't add too much detail.

He smiled again. She shook her head. He had a sexy

smile, but she had to concentrate on her report. Both of them sat in silence writing things down from memory.

When she finished, she stood up and stretched. She saw a coffee station and headed to it. She poured two cups of coffee and added cream to both, then headed back to Pete.

"Here you go." She handed him a cup.

"Thank you, Elena. Here's my report."

She sat next to him after handing him her report. She read over his. He had all the details needed. Even though his story was a little different, since he was missing in action until the very end, he had everything right.

"You did good, Pete."

"I left out all the pertinent details about us, though."

"Thank you."

"I'm sorry I let you down, Elena."

"What? You didn't let me down, Pete." She touched his thigh.

"You went through a lot before I came on scene."

"You came at exactly the right moment, Pete. I learned something through all this, though."

"What's that?"

"I can't do everything alone. I need a partner and I need to learn to trust my partner."

"God said you learned that."

"What else did he say?"

"I had been worried about the powers I had lost, but He said I had enough."

She reached out and cupped his face in her free hand.

"Yes, you did." She pulled him close and kissed him.

I still want to keep you.

Her phone pinged. She set her coffee down on a nearby table. Unplugging her phone, she scrolled down the texts she had missed.

The first few were from her family. She texted everyone that she was fine and stuck in paradise with a handsome man. *That will give them something to wonder about.*

She glanced up and saw Taggert coming toward them.

"Did you get those reports done?" Taggert asked.

"Yes, but we need copies for our department as well," she said.

"I'll get those done now." He and Pete walked up to the front desk.

She called the shelters that had been given to her to try. Only one had some room left. She joined Taggert and Pete at the front desk.

"The All Saints Cathedral is near here, Pete. We can stay there tonight."

Taggert handed her the copies and kept the originals.

"I'll get you a cab," the front desk agent said.

"Thank you."

She gave Taggert her number again, in case he needed more information.

"Let me know when you get a plane out of here," she said.

When they arrived at the Cathedral, a priest walked toward them. There were a lot of people milling about the pews. There was no Mass going on, but a lot of socializing.

"Hello, welcome." An elderly priest reached out to shake their hands.

"I'm Father Tony." He smiled. He had a strong, firm handshake.

"I'm Pete Cummings and this is Elena Romero. We're detectives from Miami, stranded here."

"Bless you both. Come on in. We will be serving a soup supper in the basement shortly, if you're hungry."

"Thank you, Father," she said.

She sat next to Pete in a pew in the back and watched the priest in the crowd, talking with people. She remembered the times she had gone to Mass with her parents and sisters. After she moved out, she went a few times, meeting her parents there, but eventually, her work schedule prevented her from going regularly. She had the urge to speak to the priest and have him hear her confession. She couldn't remember the last time she had gone and recently, she had a lot to confess. If she didn't go now, she would never do it.

"I'll be right back, Pete." She stood and moved up the aisle to where Father Tony was standing.

"Father Tony?"

"Yes?"

"Do you have time to hear a confession?"

"Of course. Come this way." He led her to the confessionals on the left side of the alter.

Once inside, she made the sign of the cross. "Bless me father, for I have sinned."

Pete sat alone, watching the people conversing with each other. They had just gone through a tragic event but their demeanor showed otherwise. Humans were more resilient than he had remembered. He watched Elena and the priest go inside a confessional.

His life was at a crossroads now. He could remain an angel and serve the Lord. But would he regain his powers? Or he can remain human, with the powers he still possessed and be Elena's partner. Could he still serve the Lord in that capacity?

— *Yes.* —

How so?

*— **Fighting evil that affects other humans and teaching them how to fight spiritually.** —*

Thank you, Lord.

He saw Elena come out of the confessional and sit at a pew up front. She prayed a long time before returning to him.

Father Tony stood at the altar and announced that supper would be served shortly.

Elena joined him just as the group followed the priest down to the basement. She grabbed his hand and hung on until they got to the table.

They found a couple seats together and chatted with the people sitting with them. The soup was good and filling.

"I think I'm going to help them clean up," she said.

"I'll help, too."

Once everyone was finished, he searched for Father Tony, while picking up the empty paper bowls and plastic utensils. He needed to clear his conscience as well.

Father Tony was listening to some children telling stories. When the children finished, he asked to speak to Father Tony alone.

She finished with the others and realized she hadn't seen Pete in a while. She headed back to the church and saw Pete talking to Father Tony in the back, where she and Pete had staked out a couple seats. By the time she reached them, Father Tony was leaving.

"Elena, there's something I want to tell you."

"What's that?" She hoped he hadn't decided to go back to being an angel. Her heart skipped a beat at the thought.

He stood before her, studying her face. Then he reached for her hands. He ran his fingers across her knuckles. She still wore the wedding rings from the first night on the ship.

"I don't think I can just be your partner."

26

H er face looked crestfallen. Tears welled up in her eyes. He still held onto her hands and got down on one knee.

"I don't want to just be your partner, I want you to be my wife, Elena. My partner for life."

Her mouth dropped open. "Yes! Yes, I want to be your wife. I love you."

He stood and pulled her into his arms, hugging her fiercely. He felt her arms reach around his back and pull him close. His heart swelled. He manifested some rings and pulled away to show them to her.

"What do you think?"

"Oh, my! I love them. But what about the ones I'm wearing?"

He blinked and the rings were gone.

"These are better."

"You mean bigger, don't you? I'm glad you made one for you, too."

"Would you rather have a smaller diamond?"

"Uh, no. This is perfect. I love them."

He helped her put the diamond on.

"These will have to wait until the ceremony." He put the two wedding bands into his pocket.

There was loud clapping coming from the altar area. When he looked up, everyone stood up front and watched the two of them.

"Do they know?" she asked.

"I think they do, now. Father Tony said he would marry us in the morning, if you want?"

"I'd like that very much." A tear escaped down her cheek. He caught it with his finger. "We'll come back here for our honeymoon after the place recovers from this hurricane. What do you say?"

"I say we come back here for our anniversary and make the most of this for our honeymoon."

He hugged her tight. When he caught Father Tony's gaze, he nodded. Everyone moved to the pews and found places to sleep. Father Tony and another man handed out blankets, aisle by aisle, until everyone had a blanket.

They lay in the last pew, head to head.

"Good night Pete. I love you."

"Good night Elena. I love you, too."

The next morning, everyone was awake and preparing for the wedding ceremony. Some of the women helped Elena get ready. They found combs for her hair. A few women gathered flowers from the outside the church and some from the vases inside. One woman handed her a white chorus gown.

"Ah, yes. This is better than these dirty clothes." She probably smelled, too. It had been a couple days since she bathed. She slipped the gown over her clothes. Another woman gathered her hair up off her neck and fixed it with combs.

Women prepared a cake in the kitchen and others fixed a reception breakfast, since no one had eaten.

"I need to borrow your phone and camera," Pete said.

She realized she had no way to charge her phone again, but since she hadn't used it much since yesterday, it still had a good charge left. She handed it to him.

When she was ready, she entered the front of the church. Someone played a piano as she walked in and down the aisle. It was beautiful music, but she didn't recognize the tune.

Pete stood at the altar with Father Tony and a deacon she had met the night before.

All the attendees were the same people who shared a meal and the pews the night before.

She gave herself to Pete, since her parents weren't there, and Father Tony united them in marriage before God and all the congregation of the All Saints Cathedral.

"Let's join in celebration with a breakfast reception in the basement," the deacon said.

"Reception?" Pete asked.

"Yes. The people wanted to do this. Just play along," Elena whispered.

There were eggs, bacon, cake, and punch. Salsa music was blaring in the background.

"You owe me a dance, I believe," she said. She pulled Pete to his feet. A slow song played. He held her in his arms, like ballroom dancing. She had only danced like that with her father, but she remembered some of the steps. It was a waltz.

"You surprised me. I didn't know you could dance like this," she said.

"I just learned."

"Wow. This is going to be an interesting marriage. Can you pass on knowledge to others?"

"Only if you want it."

When the dance ended, she and Pete cut the cake. She fed him a slice and he fed her. When she got back to the table, a man came up and handed her the phone and camera.

"I hope you enjoy these," he said.

Her phone and camera? She had forgotten Pete had borrowed them. She glanced at the photos and realized the man had taken pictures of the wedding and the reception. A tear slid down her face.

"What's wrong?" Pete joined her at the table.

"Nothing." She showed him some of the pictures. "This is the happiest day of my life."

27

H er phone rang. It was Taggert.

"Hello?"

"Romero, I just got word from the Miami bureau. They're sending a plane to pick us up. It should be here in the morning."

"Where do you want us to meet you?"

"We'll get a cab and pick you both up at 0800 hours tomorrow."

"We'll be ready. You know where we are?"

"All Saints Cathedral, right?"

"Yes."

"See you two tomorrow."

"Who was that?" Pete asked.

"Taggert. They will pick us up tomorrow at 0800 hours. We'll be on a plane for Miami after that."

"I guess we better get this honeymoon going, then, right?"

She laughed. "Do you actually know what that is?"

"Not really, no."

"Well, it involves alone time." She pulled him close and whispered in his ear. "And a lot of sex." His eyes grew wide.

"I guess we better get started." He stood and reached for her hand.

"Uh, where do you plan on taking me?"

"Let's take a walk."

She removed the gown and handed it to one of the ladies and joined Pete outside the church. They found their way down to the beach and walked along the shore.

"That water is so tempting," she said.

"What do you mean?"

"Wouldn't you like to go swimming? To bathe in a warm tub with bubble bath and just soak all this dirt and grime off you?"

He glanced at the water and then at her. Then he smiled that sexy smile and blinked. Their clothes were gone. She jumped into the water and he joined her.

"What were you thinking?" She popped up out of the water.

"How I wanted to see you naked in the water."

"Someone could have seen us," she said.

He glanced around. "No one here but us."

He pulled her close and kissed her. Then they splashed and played in the water.

After a while, they stepped out of the ocean and he blinked some dry clothes on both of them. She pulled her hair into a twisted bun and held it in place with the combs the women had given her.

"Just wait until I get you alone in my bed," she said.

"How long is that?"

"Well, I don't know. But our honeymoon is just getting started."

"I'm enjoying it already."

"I like this dress you put on me."

"It's a sundress, like the one you wore on the ship. I like it on you."

She reached up and kissed him. "Thank you."

"What do we do until tomorrow?"

"Let's explore this island," she said.

They headed back to the church to gather their things. Elena grabbed her phone and called for a cab. There was barely a charge left on it.

"Someone will be here shortly," she said.

He slipped the camera over his shoulder and grabbed the papers they needed to turn in to her captain. He folded them and tucked them into his back pocket.

She slipped her phone into her purse.

The cab took them into San Juan. Before getting out, he asked the driver for recommendations on a place to eat.

After walking around, taking pictures and just being together, they headed to the restaurant the cab driver recommended.

"This is lovely," she said. They sat at a nice table in a quiet spot of the restaurant. Business was bustling due to the hurricane and power outages in some places. The downtown area had been spared. Most of the damage was in the interior of the island. But since the hotels were full, the businesses did well in spite of the damage in other places.

When they were finished eating, Elena called for a cab to return them to the Cathedral.

"This will be an unusual wedding night, but I promise to make it up to you." She poked him in the chest.

"I will hold you to it."

28

She waved good-bye to the parishioners and headed outside.

Taggert held the door of the cab open for them.

"Here, take a picture of the two of us," Pete said. He handed her camera to Taggert.

"Make sure you get the church in the background," she said.

"What's this? A souvenir of your stay in Puerto Rico?" Taggert asked.

"Something like that," she said, smiling for the camera.

When they climbed inside the cab, Taggert glanced at her hand. He reached for her arm.

"What's this?" He held her left hand. "I know you weren't wearing a rock like this before."

She pulled her hand free and glanced at Pete. "We got married."

"Just now?"

"Yesterday," Pete said.

Taggert closed the back door and hopped inside beside the

driver. "I thought you were undercover and just pretending to be married."

"We were," she said.

"So, how long have you known each other?"

She glanced at Pete. "A few days."

Pete nodded and smiled.

Taggert scratched his head. "I hope you two know what you're doing."

She sat very close to Pete and held his hand in her lap. She knew it was a short period of time, but it felt right. Her heart was lighter today and she was happy.

"Where are the other two agents?" Pete asked.

"They went on ahead to let the pilots know we will be taking you back with us, along with Ernesto and the two bodies."

"I can't wait to get back home," Pete said. He smiled at her.

She winked at him. "I can't wait to get into a nice hot bubble bath and just soak." She pulled Pete's hand to her heart.

"You two haven't had a bath in a couple days, have you?" Taggert asked.

"Not since we left the ship. Speaking of which, our belongings are still on it."

"Check at the Port Authority when you get back. The ship will probably have your stuff in storage. I had them hold ours as well." Taggert said.

Once on board the plane, they sat near the other two agents.

"Don't forget to give us copies of your prints," Taggert said, pointing at the camera.

She and Pete settled in for the long trip. Pete couldn't get comfortable until she showed him how to adjust his seat.

When they arrived at the Miami International Airport, she breathed a sigh of relief. They were home. Taggert gave them a ride to the Port Authority, where they collected their belongings.

"Now, we find your truck," she said.

It didn't take long. They loaded their stuff into the back seat and before she could open the door, Pete was there to help her up.

"Do you think we can put another step on this side for me?"

"We'll see."

They headed to her townhouse.

"I think we need to remove these rings before going back to work," she said.

"Why?"

"Because the captain won't let us work together since we're married."

"We work well together."

"Yes, we do. Maybe we can ease into this another way and still work together."

"Have you got a plan?"

"I'm working on one, yes."

"First, we honeymoon, then we go back to work." Pete waggled his eyebrows.

She leaned over and kissed him. "I like the way you think."

29

They settled in from their trip, once they arrived at her townhouse. The first order of business was a long soak in the tub. Then they spent the next twenty-four hours, making up for lost time. She kept her promise to Pete. Several times.

Reality hit on the second day when she realized she had to buy groceries. Even that was an adventure with an angel.

Adjusting to married life was not as hard as she thought it would be. Pete came without a lot of baggage, literally. Having to cook for two people was the most challenging thing she had to overcome.

She promised the captain she would have a report for him when she got back, but she didn't mean immediately. She phoned her family with her good news first, but told them to keep it under wraps. On the third day, when she phoned the captain, he was not happy.

"I thought you were bringing me the report when you returned," he said.

She held the phone away from her ear. He was louder than usual.

"I have the report, sir, but you did say I had some time off coming to me. I took the time off first. I'll bring the report to you tomorrow morning."

"See that you do." He hung up.

"Well, it's back to the old routine tomorrow," she said.

"How long does a honeymoon last?" Pete asked.

She stood and joined him in the kitchen. "As long as we want."

"I like that." He handed her a cup of coffee.

"Thank you."

He took a sip of his coffee.

"We'll be back to work as Romero and Cummings, starting tomorrow," she said. "We'll leave our rings at home when we go to work."

"So by day we are crime fighters and by night we are honeymooners?"

"I like that. Crime fighters by day. But instead of honeymooners, let's go with lovers by night."

"That's even better."

End

BAILEY'S IRISH DREAM

Bailey Jackson had the dream again. The same erotic dream she'd had for the past year. She glanced at the passenger beside her. Hopefully, she hadn't talked in her sleep.

When the Aer Lingus jet landed at the Shannon Airport, she was anxious to get to her destination in Limerick. There, she would start the search for her dream lover, unofficially of course. After all, she was in Ireland to do research for her book.

She went through Customs and exchanged her money for Euros. Then she located the bus that would take her to her first stop.

Hopping a bus to Limerick, she pulled out her notebook and jotted down thoughts about the countryside. This would do for a start. Writing a romance about a couple in Ireland needed descriptions and impressions of people and places.

When the bus finally pulled to her stop, she disembarked and headed to the hotel.

"Welcome to our property, Ms. Jackson. What brings you to Limerick?" the front desk agent asked. He had a thick Irish brogue that lilted when he spoke.

Surprised by the question, she hesitated to answer. The dream was the real reason she was here, but the agent didn't need to know that.

"I'm here to do research," she said finally.

"Are you researching your ancestors, then?"

She read his name tag. "No, Cormac, I'm doing research for a book." But the thought of researching her ancestors was an excuse she could use later.

"What kind of book?" Cormac pushed the folio in front of her and handed her a pen.

"Romance," she whispered. She signed the form and handed it back to Cormac.

"Ahh, then I hope you find what you're looking for," he said.

"Me, too, Cormac." A second chance at love would be nice, too, she thought. She smiled.

Cormac handed her the keys and directed her to the elevator.

Researching her book was the excuse she had given her three adult children before leaving Tennessee.

"Mom, I really don't think you should be going to Ireland by yourself," her daughter had said.

"Don't you think it's a little early to be doing this? You know, so soon after Dad…died" her youngest son had said.

"How long will you be gone?" her eldest son asked when he realized he couldn't change her mind.

She balanced her suitcase, camera bag, computer bag and purse while pressing the button on the elevator.

Being married to a verbally abusive man for over twenty-six years kept the woman she was from becoming the woman she wanted to be.

The elevator doors opened. She watched as people poured out.

Besides, her husband had been dead for a year now, and while he was alive, she spent her energy defending herself against his abusive language and trying to keep a positive attitude. Since his death, she found more time and energy to write and be creative.

She stepped inside the elevator and selected her floor as the doors closed on her past. Now was the best time for her to be in Ireland. Besides, she wouldn't be alone the whole time. She would join her friend, Kay, and travel around Ireland while researching her book, and secretly watching for the man who had haunted her dreams.

Unpacking in her room, she decided the weather was chilly for May, so she pulled out a sweater and some blue jeans. After freshening up and changing clothes, she headed down to the lobby to find a place to eat.

Cormac was still at the desk and he directed her to a pub within walking distance. She took a deep breath and headed toward O'Malley's. Eating alone in a public place was a new experience for her. In the past, she had prepared meals for her family and eaten at home or eaten out with friends. She was hungry and she had to get over this fear. She had to.

O'Malley's dimly lit interior exposed large beams of mahogany-stained wood in between dark panels in the ceiling, held up by similar pillars throughout. Odd pieces of antiques decorated the hunter green walls. Several tables and chairs filled the space between the door and the L-shaped bar.

She planted herself on a barstool at the short end, near the wall, before taking time to glance around the place. Americans sat at a few tables, while a couple at the bar seemed to have Irish accents. She glanced at her watch and realized it was 10:00 a.m. The time difference would eventually catch up to her, but she wouldn't waste her first day in Ireland, sleeping.

"What'll you have, miss?" The bartender asked.

"Are you still serving breakfast?"

"Of course," he said. He handed her a menu. "Are you real hungry?"

"I'm starving," she said. She glanced over the menu.

"Then I'd recommend a full Irish breakfast. Really filling. Have you had one yet?"

"No, but it sounds good. I'll try that and a cup of coffee, too."

"I'll be right back," he said. He scooped up the menu and left.

He was back in no time with the coffee. After a few sips, she glanced down the long end of the bar and noticed a couple of men coming out of a door. An auburn-headed young woman stood between them, glancing up at a dark-haired man. They carried on a conversation.

She nearly choked on her coffee when she realized who the familiar, dark-haired man was. He had bits of gray running through his hair. His profile was handsome. Her pulse quickened at the thought that this man resembled her dream lover.

When the Irish couple at the middle of the bar stood to leave, the three at the end turned their attention to the couple. She noticed the familiar-looking man gazing in her direction. She caught her bottom lip in her teeth, trying to subdue a smile. *Was he looking at her? Had she imagined that smile?* No, he had glanced at the couple. Perhaps he knew them. She would have to save her imagination for her book-writing. Her life was not that exciting.

Moments after the couple left, the three shook hands and the mysterious man left. What if this was her only chance to meet him? Her heart pounded in her chest. No. She would not chase after a man. She had not done that in any of her dreams and she wouldn't do it now. Besides, what if he was married? The other man and woman who had been with him went back through the door they exited earlier.

Glancing around the pub, she realized it was similar to the one in her dreams. The bartender placed the food in front of her.

"Wow, that's a lot of food," she said. She picked up her fork. The eggs and blood sausage alone would have been plenty, but there were bacon, tomatoes, mushrooms, brown bread and scones. This meal would have to suffice for the rest of the day.

Michael Shaunnessy stopped by the Cathedral on his way back to the hotel.

"Father Ambrose," he said. He reached his hand out to the priest he had known since he 'crossed over.'

"Michael, what brings you to Limerick?" He directed Michael to a row of pews.

"Business, Father. I'm searching for a location for Patrick's Vetery. And, well, a means to obtain funds for opening the clinic." He sat down and leaned one arm over the back of the pew.

"And have you had any luck?" Father asked.

"O'Malley's offered to help with the fund-raising banquet. He said he'd find a location here in Limerick. I've got a few more people to contact before I go home."

"Ahh, and I bet Fionnuala will help as well."

Michael nodded. Fionnuala was the one person he didn't want to run into while he was here. But calling on O'Malley was a package deal. He sat up and crossed his arms over his chest. When William O'Malley was involved in something lucrative, his daughter Fionnuala wanted in on it.

"Have you had more dreams, Michael?" Father asked.

"Since we last talked, yes, but now I know they weren't dreams, Father."

"No?"

"They were premonitions. I believe they will happen, just the way I described them to you."

"And how do you know this, Michael?"

"I saw her. She's real, and right here in Limerick."

ABOUT THE AUTHOR

To keep up to date on the author's book releases, and to get the FREE "Vaedra Chronicles" companion book, please join

Ester's Readers Group at:

www.esterlopez.com
Follow Ester's blogs at:
www.esterlopez.com
www.authorblogspot.esterlopez.com
Follow Ester on:
www.facebook.com/EsterLopezAuthor
or on Twitter at:
www.twitter.com/esterlopez1
And if you like the story, please leave an honest review at
your favorite bookseller
You can also join Ester's Group Page on Facebook at
Virtual Book Signing & Takeover Group